A FLIGHT TO HEAVEN

Chiara then looked up to see a flock of great white swans flying with their long necks stretched out and their wings beating swiftly.

"Oh, you are just so beautiful!" she cried, as they sped past her like white arrows, the sun shining on their feathers. "Wait! Where are you going?"

She gathered up her skirts and ran after the swans, leaping over clumps of grass as she struggled to keep up.

'I will never catch them,' she thought, 'they are so wild and free, but I cannot bear to lose sight of them.'

Ahead of her, she could see a mirror-like expanse of water, where one field had flooded with the winter rain and she gasped with delight as the swans turned in the sky and headed for the water. They were going to land there!

She then threw her hood back and stood, panting, to watch them, one by one, as they splashed down onto the water, legs waving and just for a moment she thought that they looked rather clumsy.

But next they ruffled and tidied their feathers and then they were gliding serenely over the water, their lovely necks arched and their proud eyes gazing all around.

THE BARBARA CARTLAND
PINK COLLECTION

Titles in this series

A FLIGHT TO HEAVEN

BARBARA CARTLAND

Barbaracartland.com Ltd

THE BARBARA CARTLAND PINK COLLECTION

Dame Barbara Cartland is still regarded as the most prolific bestselling author in the history of the world.

In her lifetime she was frequently in the Guinness Book of Records for writing more books than any other living author.

Her most amazing literary feat was to double her output from 10 books a year to over 20 books a year when she was 77 to meet the huge demand.

She went on writing continuously at this rate for 20 years and wrote her very last book at the age of 97, thus completing an incredible 400 books between the ages of 77 and 97.

Her publishers finally could not keep up with this phenomenal output, so at her death in 2000 she left behind an amazing 160 unpublished manuscripts, something that no other author has ever achieved.

Barbara's son, Ian McCorquodale, together with his daughter Iona, felt that it was their sacred duty to publish all these titles for Barbara's millions of admirers all over the world who so love her wonderful romances.

So in 2004 they started publishing the 160 brand new Barbara Cartlands as *The Barbara Cartland Pink Collection*, as Barbara's favourite colour was always pink – and yet more pink!

The Barbara Cartland Pink Collection is published monthly exclusively by Barbaracartland.com and the books are numbered in sequence from 1 to 160.

Enjoy receiving a brand new Barbara Cartland book each month by taking out an annual subscription to the Pink Collection, or purchase the books individually.

The Pink Collection is available from the Barbara Cartland website www.barbaracartland.com via mail order and through all good bookshops.

In addition Ian and Iona are proud to announce that The Barbara Cartland Pink Collection is now available in ebook format as from Valentine's Day 2011.

For more information, please contact us at:

Barbaracartland.com Ltd.
Camfield Place
Hatfield
Hertfordshire AL9 6JE
United Kingdom

Telephone: +44 (0)1707 642629
Fax: +44 (0)1707 663041
Email: info@barbaracartland.com

THE LATE DAME BARBARA CARTLAND

Barbara Cartland who sadly died in May 2000 at the age of nearly 99 was the world's most famous romantic novelist who wrote 723 books in her lifetime with worldwide sales of over 1 billion copies and her books were translated into 36 different languages.

As well as romantic novels, she wrote historical biographies, 6 autobiographies, theatrical plays, books of advice on life, love, vitamins and cookery. She also found time to be a political speaker and television and radio personality.

She wrote her first book at the age of 21 and this was called *Jigsaw*. It became an immediate bestseller and sold 100,000 copies in hardback and was translated into 6 different languages. She wrote continuously throughout her life, writing bestsellers for an astonishing 76 years. Her books have always been immensely popular in the United States, where in 1976 her current books were at numbers 1 & 2 in the B. Dalton bestsellers list, a feat never achieved before or since by any author.

Barbara Cartland became a legend in her own lifetime and will be best remembered for her wonderful romantic novels, so loved by her millions of readers throughout the world.

Her books will always be treasured for their moral message, her pure and innocent heroines, her good looking and dashing heroes and above all her belief that the power of love is more important than anything else in everyone's life.

*"When I am kissed by the man I love and who loves me,
I always fly to Heaven and it is so beautiful I want
to stay there for ever!"*

Barbara Cartland

CHAPTER ONE
1903

Lady Chiara Fairfax had never felt quite so cold in all her life as the chaise came to a halt in front of a tall Georgian house that stood not far from the towering spires of Ely Cathedral.

Shivering, she stepped down from the chaise onto the cobbles of the little street that wound its way up to the great Cathedral.

It was just teatime, but the sun was already low on the horizon and black storm clouds were blowing across the darkening sky.

A heavy drenching rain began to fall, but Chiara felt glad, as if she waited in the street for a few moments, the raindrops on her face would hide the fact that she had been crying.

It was so kind of her best friend, Elizabeth, to invite her to stay and she did not want to arrive looking utterly miserable.

But she simply could not help it.

All through the long drive from her home, Rensham Hall in Norfolk, she could not forget that her darling Papa was dead and that her Mama had sent her away, telling her,

"Chiara, my angel, I cannot bear to see you looking so sad. You must go and spend some time with someone of your own age and try to laugh again and be happy."

The blue front door of the Georgian house flew open and a tall girl with a glorious mane of red-gold curls came bounding down the stone steps, a beaming smile of welcome on her face.

"Chiara! My dearest, dearest friend in the whole world! What are you doing standing out here in the rain?"

Elizabeth must have been watching out for Chiara from her bedroom window overlooking the street.

She threw her arms around Chiara in a joyful hug.

"Oh, I am so glad to see you. There is so much to tell you. But you, poor thing, must come inside at once."

Elizabeth then seized Chiara's hand and pulled her up the steps and into the warm brightly lit hall.

"I did not think that I would be seeing you again so soon," she said, as she helped Chiara out of her damp cloak and led her into the parlour.

The two girls had attended a renowned school for Young Ladies in Cambridge and they had finished their studies a few weeks ago before Christmas.

"I just wish it was not such a sad reason that brings you here," Elizabeth said, her bright face suddenly worried. "I know how much you loved your Papa."

Chiara sat beside Elizabeth on the sofa in front of a crackling fire and wiped her hand over her wet cheeks to push away any lingering tears.

"Yes, I did – so very much," she managed to say, although her voice felt weak and shaky.

Lord Fairfax had loved Chiara too.

He had fallen deeply in love with Chiara's Mama, quite late in his life, when all his Society friends believed that he would remain a bachelor for ever.

But the beautiful young Italian dancer, Signorina Minotti, had stolen his heart completely and, to the outrage of his family and friends, he had married her and embarked on twenty years of blissful happiness.

Chiara was their only child and he adored her. She was an enchanting girl, graceful and dark-haired like her Mama and shared her talents and she could dance and sing almost as soon as she could walk.

"Look at you, my darling baby! You are just like a little fairy," Lord Fairfax would say to her in his deep voice, rumbling with laughter as Chiara tried to pull him to his feet so that he could dance with her.

"Well I never, Baby Chiara," he would exclaim, as he balanced precariously on one foot and raised the other in the air in imitation of his daughter. "Who would think to see an old gentleman like myself taking part in a ballet?"

But that was a long time ago.

Chiara was seventeen now, quite grown up, and due to be presented at Court later in the year.

And her dear Papa was no more.

Elizabeth reached out and took Chiara's hand.

"Poor Chiara!" she sighed. "We will do everything we can to make you comfortable here. Sit by the fire and get warm and I will go and see about tea."

"Elizabeth – you are so kind – " Chiara murmured, as her friend leapt up from the sofa. "But wait, you said you had something to tell me. Whatever is it?"

Elizabeth's cheeks flushed softly pink.

"Oh – I'll tell you later. Tea is more important."

And she hurried away to speak to the cook.

Chiara lay back on the sofa cushions and closed her eyes, as her frozen hands came painfully back to life in the warmth from the fire.

But nothing could touch the icy pain that filled her heart.

She now thought back to the last time she had been happy. School had just finished and Chiara, together with two large trunks and an assortment of bags and boxes, was bowling through the Norfolk countryside in the beautiful Fairfax family coach.

The wintry sun shone down over the patchwork of fields and hedges and her heart had swelled with joy as she saw the graceful outline of Rensham Hall appear on the top of a low hill.

She had smiled to herself as she peered out of the coach window. It was only in Norfolk that anyone would think of Rensham Hall as being on top of a hill.

It was really more of a slight rise in the landscape, but Norfolk was so low-lying that any small bump that was not completely flat was always described as a hill.

Rensham Hall was built of pale yellow stone, which always seemed full of light, even on a dull day and it stood in the middle of a beautiful Park with wide acres of grass and many tall trees with spreading branches.

"Oh, quick, quick!" Chiara whispered, longing for the horses to break into a gallop, as they clattered through the gates and trotted up the long drive to Rensham Hall.

Her heart was beating as she jumped down from the coach and ran up the front steps and into the empty hall.

"I'm back!" she called out and could not help but spin round in a joyous pirouette, her skirt billowing out around her like the petals of a flower.

It was so good to be home, to see the great vase of yellow jasmine and winter honeysuckle that her Mama had placed on the round table at the foot of the stairs.

To smell the delicious mix of lavender wax, pipe tobacco and sweet gardenia that always lingered in the hall.

And now the scent of pipe tobacco was growing stronger.

"Is that my Chiara? My baby girl?" Lord Fairfax's voice called out from the landing at the top of the stairs.

"Who else! Of course it's me, Papa!"

Lord Fairfax's tall body, stooped at the shoulders now, as he was a very old man, was approaching down the wide staircase.

He was wearing a heavy velvet dressing gown and Chiara was surprised to see that he was holding onto the banisters with his right hand. She could never remember seeing him do that before.

In his other hand he held his briarwood pipe and curling from its bowl was the sweet-scented smoke that she loved so much and on his grey-whiskered face was a smile of pure delight.

It was just another perfect homecoming. She stood at the foot of the stairs, smiling up at him, absolutely happy to be back home again.

"Chiara!" her Mama's sweet voice rang out behind her. "*Mia cara*! You are home, how wonderful!"

There was a light tap of heels over the marble floor and then Mama's gardenia scent filled Chiara's nose.

Next her arms were around her in a passionate hug.

"And now you are home with us for good," she said, stroking Chiara's shining dark hair. "Until, of course, we find a handsome beau for you – "

"Mama! I have only just walked through the door and already you are trying to marry me off!"

Lady Fairfax's dark eyes glowed with mischief.

"Oh – to be so young again," she sighed. "You are going to have so much fun, *cara*." She turned and looked up at the staircase. "But look, Chiara – here is Papa! Oh, careful, my darling love, *be careful*!"

Lord Fairfax seemed rather unsteady. His slippered foot caught on the carpet and his tall body wavered.

Lady Fairfax stepped swiftly towards him, but then suddenly his legs gave way beneath him and he fell heavily forward, tumbling awkwardly down the last few stairs and landing at Chiara's feet.

"Papa!" she cried, bending over him.

His grey eyes stared up at her and a smile twitched on his thin lips.

"Why did you come downstairs? What were you thinking of? The doctor advised you to stay in your room."

Lady Fairfax pushed Chiara aside and seized her husband's shoulder.

"What have you done to yourself? Oh, my darling, you are hurt!"

Lord Fairfax lay motionless on the marble tiles. His eyes were wide open, gazing up at the painted ceiling.

"No, no, no!" Lady Fairfax's voice rose in a shrill wail of fear, as she cried out to her husband in Italian, begging him to wake up, to speak to her.

Suddenly servants appeared, the housekeeper and the parlourmaids bringing water and towels and a bottle of brandy and a stocky footman, who said he would send for the doctor straight away.

But it was too late. Old Lord Fairfax heard nothing of the hubbub around him, saw nothing of the wife who stroked his face with her slender hand, felt nothing of the warm tears that splashed onto his face.

He had died from a sudden heart attack.

Chiara shivered in the warm parlour, as she recalled those awful moments, her Mama's cries of despair and the terrible chill that crept into her heart when she understood that her beloved Papa was no more.

"Now then, we have tea and fruitcake and cook has given me some muffins we can toast ourselves!"

Elizabeth had returned, carrying a large tray piled high with good things.

Chiara picked up the toasting fork and speared a fat muffin on the end of it, so that she could hold it next to the red embers at the bottom of the fire.

The wonderful smell of the toasting muffin and the taste of the hot tea made her feel a little better.

"Goodness, these are doing very quickly!" she said, passing a nicely browned and crisp muffin to Elizabeth. "What is the news you were going to tell me?"

Elizabeth gave a little sigh, as she spread butter and jam over her muffin.

"Oh, Chiara! I have met a young man – Arthur! He is staying in Ely with some relatives."

Her cheeks had turned pink.

"Elizabeth! So what is he like? Do your parents know about him?"

Chiara had never seen her friend look quite like this before, so shy and secretive and yet proud at the same time.

"I haven't told them yet and he is quite marvellous, so handsome. He is an Officer in the Royal Navy."

"But what will your Papa say?" Chiara asked.

Elizabeth's father was the Dean of Ely Cathedral and a most important figure in the town.

"I am going to tell him tonight after Evensong and then, if he agrees, Arthur might come and pay us a visit tomorrow and you could meet him, Chiara."

Chiara felt a little stab of pain in her heart. She was so cold and sad and empty now next to Elizabeth, who was glowing with excitement and happiness.

"And you never know, Chiara!" she was saying, "perhaps Arthur might know of a fellow Officer who could be your beau."

Chiara shook her head.

"I don't think so," she said, "I just cannot imagine that I will ever – " and her voice shook as she felt tears coming into her eyes again.

"Oh, I'm so sorry! Of course the last thing you will want to do is start thinking about young men, when you feel so miserable. Don't give it another thought. Will you come to the Cathedral for Evensong, Chiara?"

"I think I would rather just rest."

Chiara did not think she could face the vast cold Cathedral with its echoing aisles and great ribbed ceiling, even though she loved to hear the choir singing.

Elizabeth took her upstairs to a pretty blue-painted bedroom and told her to lie down for just as long as she wanted.

It was dark outside now and the rain had stopped, and through the open curtains Chiara could see a single star shining down over the higgledy-piggledy roofs of the town.

She lay for a long time, watching the tiny point of light against the darkness and somehow it comforted her.

'I *will* be happy again,' she told herself. 'I cannot see how, but I will.'

With a tiny glimmer of hope in her heart, Chiara turned over in the bed and then fell into the first deep and peaceful sleep she had enjoyed since her Papa had passed away.

*

Count Arkady Dimitrov turned away from the buzz of conversation and the clink of glasses in the drawing room of the fine house he had rented in Mayfair.

Outside the tall bay window the street below was quiet and the pavements gleamed wet from heavy rain.

It was a far cry from the outstanding prospect over the River Neva that stretched away outside his Palace in St. Petersburg.

Everything in London seemed to him so small by comparison. Small and rather drab, like this house, that the agent had assured him was one of the best to be found with all its furniture and fittings brand new and in the very latest style.

The Count gave a wry little smile.

This drawing room was intensely bland, he thought, remembering all the gilded chairs, the great gold clock, the embroidered draperies of his own fabulous salon at home.

And it was impossible to obtain decent caviar here in London. Not that his guests complained. They would happily nibble on tiny sandwiches of thin white bread and cucumber!

A woman's hand touched his arm.

"You are very thoughtful tonight, Count. Will you not share your musings with us?"

It was Mrs. Fulwell, a fair-haired English widow who had been very helpful throughout the Count's stay in London, inviting him to dinner parties and the theatre and making sure that he was never short of entertainment or company.

Arkady took her hand and kissed it politely, bowing low.

Mrs. Fulwell, he reflected, was looking very smart tonight with her pale hair dressed in a soft flattering style and her plump face blushing sweetly in the candlelight.

The best thing, undoubtedly, about his stay so far, had been the prettiness of the English girls.

And indeed twenty years ago, Mrs. Fulwell must have been a very fine example of a classic 'English Rose'.

But now her delicate rosy skin was showing signs of becoming lined and her hand, where it lay in his, was rather too large for Arkady's taste.

He smiled politely at the widow.

"I am just thinking of home," he told her. "I miss St. Petersburg and my country estate. I have been away for a long time."

"Oh, but it seems no time at all since you arrived here and from what you tell us, it's quite dreadfully cold in Russia at this time of year."

"Yes, indeed."

Arkady closed his eyes for a second and pictured the gleam of thick snow under the winter sky.

At least here in England you did not have to swathe yourself in furs before you stepped out of the door. He had not seen a single snowflake since his arrival in London – only what seemed like endless rain.

Perhaps it was all the moisture in the air that gave the women their exquisite soft complexions.

Mrs. Fulwell's blue eyes were gazing imploringly up at him.

"I hope you are not thinking of leaving us so soon," she said. "Why, my darling girls will be quite devastated! They are so longing to meet you."

She had mentioned her two daughters before, but he had never actually met them. They seemed to be always busy with dressmakers and milliners and a constant stream of social engagements.

Mrs. Fulwell had assured him that they were bound to be engaged very soon, as they were both so very pretty.

He turned back to the window, suddenly longing for Russia, for the fresh icy air of St. Petersburg and the brilliance of the starlit sky on a clear winter's night.

Tonight just one tiny star could be seen twinkling bravely through the hazy light of the London gas lamps.

"You are drifting away again," Mrs. Fulwell was saying, her hand still on his arm.

"Oh, forgive me," he smiled.

Perhaps, if her girls were as charming as she had obviously once been, it would be worth meeting them.

And, he thought, high above the London haze, the stars were shining just as brightly as they did over his homeland.

"St. Petersburg will wait," he said. "So I shall be delighted to stay longer in London. You must bring your daughters for some Russian tea. Perhaps tomorrow?"

Mrs. Fulwell blushed red with pleasure and made a little curtsey to the Count.

*

"Oh, you are awake!" Elizabeth was bending over Chiara, her cheeks flushed and her eyes shining.

"I have brought you some tea, look! You were fast asleep when I came to tell you that dinner was ready last night and we decided to leave you alone and let you rest."

Chiara yawned and sat up. She had been so deeply asleep that her head felt heavy and her eyelids wanted to sink down and close once more, but sunlight was shining in through the curtains and she must get up.

"I told Papa last night," Elizabeth was saying, speaking quickly in an excited state, "and he wants to meet Arthur. He has asked him to come this morning and then join us for luncheon. Oh, I do hope they get on."

Chiara sipped her tea and felt herself beginning to wake up.

"I am sure they will, Elizabeth," she murmured.

"I hope Papa will not be too fierce with him."

Elizabeth looked a little anxious. Her Papa was a tall broad-shouldered man with thick bushy brows and a mane of iron-grey hair and, in the dark clothes he wore as Dean, he could look very stern and forbidding.

"If Arthur loves you, he will not allow your Papa to upset him," Chiara suggested. "You must not worry."

She could see that Elizabeth was very nervous.

"And you must not think about me this morning," Chiara continued. "I shall take myself out for a walk – look what a beautiful day it is – and you and Arthur can spend a little time together."

"Oh, but dear Chiara! You have only just arrived. I would not dream of turning you out of the house."

Chiara shook her head.

"I am longing for some fresh air and I shall come back in good time for luncheon."

Elizabeth sighed.

"Oh, I do hope that Papa will be pleasant to Arthur. But you must be hungry. I have brought you some toast. You cannot go out without eating anything."

Since her Papa died, Chiara had no appetite at all. But she nibbled a piece of the toast to please her friend and was surprised to find that she quite enjoyed it.

There was so much sky, here in the Fen country, Chiara thought, and on a bright day like this everything seemed to shine with a bright clear light.

She was warmly wrapped in her own cloak with its fur-lined hood and Elizabeth had lent her a pair of thick gloves to keep the icy wind from her hands.

She walked through the winding streets of Ely and soon found herself at the edge of the town, looking out over a wide expanse of grass and glinting water, where the rivers and dykes ran through the fields.

There was still a long while to go before luncheon and Chiara decided to explore one of the green tracks that ran between high hedges leading out into the countryside.

Chiara walked briskly to keep warm. There was no one about on this cold day and no birds were singing.

She was just thinking that perhaps she should turn back, when she heard a strange noise in the air above her head. A sort of creaking sound, the like of which she had never heard before.

Chiara then looked up to see a flock of great white swans flying with their long necks stretched out and their wings beating swiftly.

"Oh, you are just so beautiful!" she cried, as they sped past her like white arrows, the sun shining on their feathers. "Wait! Where are you going?"

She gathered up her skirts and ran after the swans, leaping over clumps of grass as she struggled to keep up.

'I will never catch them,' she thought, 'they are so wild and free, but I cannot bear to lose sight of them.'

Ahead of her, she could see a mirror-like expanse of water, where one field had flooded with the winter rain and she gasped with delight as the swans turned in the sky and headed for the water. They were going to land there!

She then threw her hood back and stood, panting, to watch them, one by one, as they splashed down onto the water, legs waving and just for a moment she thought that they looked rather clumsy.

But next they ruffled and tidied their feathers and then they were gliding serenely over the water, their lovely necks arched and their proud eyes gazing all around.

There were five of them.

Now that she was close to the swans, Chiara could see that three of them still had some grey feathers, which meant that they were young, while the other two were both pristine brilliant white.

"Oh, you must be a family," she whispered.

The two white swans were circling close to each other, now brushing their wings intimately and suddenly they arched their beautiful necks and twined them together in a gesture of affection.

It was almost as if they were creating the shape of a heart with their necks.

Spellbound, Chiara watched them. It was the most unexpected and exquisite thing she had ever seen and she could have stayed and watched for ever.

But now the swans were separating and gliding off, dipping their heads under the water to search for food.

It was time for Chiara to go back to Elizabeth's house for luncheon and her heart sank. While she had been chasing the swans, all her sadness had disappeared.

Why could she not be like these swans, free to fly wherever she chose, living out in this glorious world of light, space and joy?

And how could she bear to feel so alone?

Watching the two adult swans caressing each other with such perfect beauty had left her with a strange pain in her heart.

'Is that what it is to love?' she thought. 'Will I ever find anyone who will touch my heart? Elizabeth has done it, but what lies in store for me?'

And with slow steps she made her way back into the town.

CHAPTER TWO

"Chiara, this is Arthur," Elizabeth said and the tall fair-haired young man who sat beside her on the sofa leapt up to greet her.

"My fiancé!" Elizabeth continued, her eyes shining with happiness.

Arthur bowed low over Chiara's hand.

"I am delighted to meet you," he said. "Elizabeth has told me so much about you

And then, as if drawn by a magnet, he was back on the sofa again, slipping his arm through Elizabeth's.

Chiara was reminded of the beautiful swans she had just seen on the Fens and how they had twined their necks together so tenderly and passionately.

"I am very very happy for you both," she sighed.

"Papa says that he has given us his blessing, but I think he might need a little while to get used to the idea," Elizabeth added with a smile.

"Not at all!" the Dean came and stood behind his daughter, resting a hand on her shoulder. "I must admit, I was taken a little by surprise, but I have spent a long time this morning talking to Arthur and I can see that you two are not only completely besotted with each other, but also very well suited and will be happy together."

Chiara's eyes stung with tears as she thought of her own Papa and how he would never see the man that she might marry and would never have the same proud look in his eyes that the Dean had now as he gazed at Elizabeth.

"Choosing the person you marry and spend the rest of your life with is the most important decision you will ever make," he said.

Arthur let go of Elizabeth's arm and sat up straight on the sofa, looking serious.

"Oh, Papa! Please don't give us one of your long sermons, not today!" Elizabeth cried, recapturing Arthur's hand. "Let's just be happy and enjoy ourselves."

"It's so easy to forget with all the excitement what a great venture you are embarking upon, becoming man and wife in the eyes of God," the Dean continued, but there was a mischievous twinkle in his grey eyes.

"And let's remember that there are serious matters to be attended to before Arthur's next leave is granted and the wedding can take place. There will be an inordinate number of dresses and other fripperies to be bought and a myriad of arrangements to be put in place."

He turned to Chiara and smiled at her.

"How fortuitous, my dear Elizabeth, that you have your friend, Chiara, at hand to help you and your Mama with the arduous task of choosing pretty clothes!"

He held out his elbow to lead Chiara into luncheon.

When they had finished eating and were leaving the table, Elizabeth said that she would like to show Arthur the garden and the shrubbery.

"There will be very little to see, my dearest, at this time of year," the Dean said.

His wife put her hand on his arm and gave him a meaningful look.

"Of course, Elizabeth, do take Arthur out for some fresh air. You can tell him about all the plants that will be coming up later on the in the spring and summer."

Elizabeth gave her Mama a grateful hug and left the dining room, her hand in Arthur's.

The Dean shook his head in disbelief as the door closed behind them.

"Why on earth would anyone want to walk around the garden on a cold day like today with nothing but bare earth and leafless stems to look at?" he asked.

"My dear, they are in love!" his wife replied. "It does not matter if the garden is completely bare. It might just as well be a hothouse full of tropical blooms for all they will notice it. They only have eyes for each other."

"Of course, you are right and I have spoken quite enough on serious matters already. Young Arthur seems a fine, sensible and well-brought up young man and I have no doubt that I can trust him to look after Elizabeth."

The Dean turned to Chiara,

"I usually take a cup of coffee in my study after luncheon. Would you care to join me?"

Chiara was surprised at this. The Dean was always such a busy man, either writing sermons or talking to his parishioners, who came to him with all their problems.

"I should love to," she replied, "but I don't want to take up your time, if you have important things to do."

The Dean smiled at her.

"And what makes you think you are not important, young lady? We have been neglecting you badly in all this excitement and that is most remiss of us."

She followed him into his study, where books not only lined the walls, but were heaped upon the chairs and even piled in towers on the floor.

Chiara moved several large volumes from the chair

that faced the Dean's desk and sat down.

"These are hard times for you," he began, "and it is always difficult for a young girl to lose her Papa."

Chiara nodded, not trusting herself to say anything.

"And you have come here to stay with us so that you can enjoy the company of your friend Elizabeth – and the thoughtless girl has gone and fallen in love and has got herself engaged!"

The Dean's eyes looked at her kindly from under his bushy brows.

"I am happy for her," Chiara replied. "It's just – "

Suddenly she found herself telling the Dean how upset she was to think that her own dear Papa would not be here to meet her own fiancé when she became engaged.

The Dean nodded.

"That is, indeed, a great pity," he said, "but is there a young man?"

Chiara was horrified to find that tears were spilling out of her eyes and running down her face.

"No, no – there is no one," she replied, struggling to control the sobs that threatened to overcome her. "I am quite sure that I will never fall in love – or that anyone will ever fall in love with me."

The Dean shook his head.

"Nonsense! You have only just suffered a terrible bereavement and you are feeling very low and sad because of it. Also it is January, the darkest time of the year. Only someone as impulsive and foolish as my dearest Elizabeth would think of falling in love in January!"

The proud look Chiara had noticed earlier returned to his face for a moment.

"I really *am* so happy for her," she said, blinking

back the tears, "and I think it will be great fun to help her with her trousseau."

"Bravely spoken, my dear. You will pull through this dark time and you are a charming girl. Very pretty indeed. You will have any number of young men pursuing you before too long. I shall be delighted to look them over for you and give my approval!"

In spite of herself, Chiara found she was laughing.

The idea of bringing all her prospective beaux to Ely to be interviewed by the Dean was very amusing.

"I shall not like any of them, I am sure!" she said. "I shall never fall in love."

The Dean's expression became serious now and he looked into her eyes.

"You must trust in Providence, my dear. Love will come to you in its own good time and, when it comes, you must welcome it and give thanks to God."

Once again Chiara was surprised. She had certainly not expected that Elizabeth's Papa would give her a lecture about love.

"But – how will I know?" she asked.

"I think you had better ask Elizabeth about that. I am sure she will have plenty to say on that subject. And now I really must think about Sunday's sermon."

He picked up a pen and began to shuffle the papers on his desk.

Chiara thanked him for speaking to her and, as she left the study, the Dean looked up at her in a steady grave way that made her suddenly feel strong and, if not actually happy, brighter than she had felt since her Papa's death.

Elizabeth met her in the hall.

"Arthur has gone," she said in a shaky voice. "He has to go back to his Regiment this afternoon. I shall not see him now for ages."

She looked flushed, as if she had been crying.

"Perhaps we should go into the town and have a look at the local shops," Chiara suggested, remembering the Dean's words before luncheon. "You are going to need so many new clothes."

Elizabeth gave a little sniff and wiped her eyes.

"There's a new shop that has just opened," she said. "Les Cygnes. It's run by a Frenchwoman and Mama says that the dresses are lovely."

"Then let's go there right away!" Chiara proposed and the two girls hurried to fetch their cloaks and gloves.

*

"So – just how big is your Palace in St. Petersburg, Count Dimitrov?" Marigold, the younger one of the Misses Fulwell, asked.

Arkady was now beginning to regret his decision to invite the very charming widow, Mrs. Fulwell, and her two daughters for Russian tea.

Marigold was most definitely the prettier of the two sisters, he surmised, with her soft round cheeks and pale blonde hair. In fact she was probably one of the prettiest girls he had met in his stay in London. But her constant questions were beginning to irritate him.

"I have never actually measured it," he replied, "but I believe that, after the Czar's residence, it is one of the finest Palaces in the City."

Marigold gave a little giggle.

"Is it as big as Buckingham Palace?" she enquired.

Arkady was saved from having to reply to this by the entrance of his impeccable English butler, Jesmond, followed by a footman carrying a large samovar.

This exquisite piece of tea-making equipment was silver, decorated with brilliant blue enamel.

The footman set it down on a small table and then a parlourmaid placed a tray of tea-glasses with pretty blue and silver handles next to the samovar.

"I hope everything is to your satisfaction, Count Dimitrov. The lemons are fresh from Covent Garden this morning and the plum jam is from the country estate of my previous employer, Lord Hunsbury," the butler stated in a low voice.

"How marvellous!" Mrs. Fulwell said, as Jesmond filled a glass from the samovar and offered it to her. "Such a treat, girls. We are going to have real Russian tea."

Eglantine, her elder daughter, with the same blonde hair as her sister, but a bit taller with high cheekbones and a long chin, looked down her nose as Jesmond asked her if she would prefer sugar or jam with her tea.

"I normally take jam with scones," the Count heard her say, although she was speaking very quietly to avoid her mother's attention. "So sugar, I suppose."

"Well, how many bedrooms does the Palace have?" Marigold persisted.

"I have no idea," Arkady replied, which was the perfect truth.

There were many rooms in his St. Petersburg home that he had never even seen. It was the job of his staff to keep them clean and beautifully decorated and he never concerned himself with such trivia.

"Marigold!" Mrs. Fulwell had gone rather pink. "Drink your tea, dear."

Marigold picked up her glass and took a sip.

"Ouch!" she squeaked. "It's so bitter!"

Jesmond was at her side at once, holding out a blue

enamel dish.

"Perhaps the young lady would care for some more sugar? The lemon can be a bit sharp if one isn't used to it."

Arkady was the last to be served and he put a very large spoonful of plum jam in his glass.

It was his favourite way to take tea, reminding him of a happy childhood on his vast country estate, where his beautiful Mama would hold court in the salon, gossiping with friends and relatives and where there was always a glass of strong tea sweetened with jam to welcome him back from one of his adventures in the countryside.

He was beginning to feel homesick for the wide open spaces of his Russian homeland. Here in London the streets were always crowded with carriages and people.

Perhaps he should take up the invitation that he had received only yesterday over dinner at Buckingham Palace.

Arkady now turned and spoke to Mrs. Fulwell.

"His Majesty the King, has invited me to visit him next month at his house in – where is it, Jesmond?"

"Norfolk, Count Dimitrov," Jesmond answered him with a bow. "The King's country house at Sandringham."

"I cannot make up my mind to go or not – "

"How lovely!" Mrs. Fulwell simpered as she took another sip of her tea and held her lips in a determined smile in spite of the lemon.

"Norfolk is very boring," Eglantine piped up. She had managed to drink all of her tea with the help of several extra spoons of sugar.

"Why is that?" Arkady quizzed her, thinking that Eglantine might be an attractive young woman, if only she would smile a little more and allow her stiff back to relax so that she could sit a little more gracefully on the sofa.

"There's nothing there," Eglantine replied. "It's flat

and very cold and goes on for miles and miles."

"Eglantine – whatever are you talking about!" Mrs. Fulwell had now turned very pink. "Norfolk is perfectly charming. Why your Uncle Mervyn is there at the moment, enjoying the finest shooting in England."

She turned to the Count.

"I am speaking of my brother, the racehorse trainer, Mr. Mervyn Hunter. Perhaps you have heard of him?"

Arkady was not listening.

Eglantine's words had conjured up a vision of the Russian Steppes, where the grassland stretched away for ever and above the glorious skies were limitless.

He gave a little sigh. He was now definitely feeling homesick.

"I think that perhaps I should take up the King's invitation," he muttered. "Ladies, would you care for some more tea?"

*

"I really must confess," Elizabeth whispered, "that actually I really hate shopping for clothes."

"I never would have guessed!" Chiara answered. "Why?"

The Proprietor of Les Cygnes, Madame Winterson, who was from Paris and had opened her little shop after her English husband had passed away, emerged from the back of the shop carrying two elegant wooden chairs.

"Sit, if you please, *mademoiselles*, and I will bring some *modes* for you to see," she suggested.

The two girls sat down and Madame Winterson disappeared again.

"Everybody thinks that red-haired girls should wear green and I really dislike green!" Elizabeth said.

"Well, then you must not have it," Chiara replied,

looking up as Madame Winterson returned, expecting her to be bringing a variety of emerald and leafy green fabrics.

But the armful of rustling silk the Frenchwoman carried was of a soft golden colour.

"These warm tones, *mademoiselle*, will perfectly complement your lovely hair. Would you care to try one?"

She held up a pretty dress, shaking out the soft bodice and the long full sleeves.

Elizabeth gave a gasp of surprise and then followed Madame Winterson into the back of the shop.

When she came back, Chiara clapped her hands in delight. The gold silk dress was in the very latest style, pulled in tightly at the waist and very loose and full over the bust and hips.

Elizabeth looked very grown-up, Chiara thought.

The elegant silhouette was so pretty that it made her look just like a proud soft-feathered pigeon as she twirled around, her long skirts sweeping over the floor.

"What do you think?" she was asking anxiously. "I have never worn anything like this before."

"It's wonderful!" Chiara cried. "You look, oh, you look like a beautiful golden dove, all ready to bill and coo with Arthur!"

"But the colour?"

"It's perfect," Chiara told her friend. "It makes your face glow and your hair look so warm and attractive."

Madame Winterson came bustling out again and this time her arms were full of russet brown velvet.

"And now, what about this?" she said and draped a little fitted coat around Elizabeth's shoulders.

"You must have it!" Chiara said. "It goes perfectly with the dress and it brings out all the brown tones in your hair. It's really lovely!"

Elizabeth looked at herself in Madame Winterson's long mirror.

"You are right! I would never have thought to wear brown, but it really suits me. Thank you, *madame*. If you put these on one side for me, I will tell Papa that I should like to buy them."

The little Frenchwoman looked very pleased.

"*De rien, mademoiselle*, and now for your friend?"

She looked at Chiara.

"Oh no, I don't need anything," Chiara said. "I am not the one who is going to be married very soon!"

Madame Winterson shook her head.

"Then we must put that right at once. I have just the creation that will bring all the young gentlemen tumbling to your feet!"

She disappeared again.

"Do let's go," Chiara urged, jumping to her feet.

But Madame Winterson was back.

She held up a little white dress, as fresh and bright as a snowflake, that was trimmed with delicate lace at the neck and round the elbow-length sleeves and wrapped at the waist with a blue silk sash.

"Oh, Chiara!" Elizabeth breathed. "It's just like a pretty white cloud."

A ray of sunshine shone through the shop window and touched the dress, lighting up the gleaming white silk.

Chiara recalled the brilliant light reflecting from the lake she had walked to and the pure gleaming whiteness of the swans' feathers as they glided over the water.

"You *must* try it on," Elizabeth was saying.

Chiara went into the back of the shop and stood behind a thick velvet curtain as the Frenchwoman helped her into the dress.

The waist was very tight and it was strange to feel the cool air on her bare forearms as she walked back out into the shop.

Now it was Elizabeth's turn to clap her hands in delight.

"It was made for you, Chiara! I can just see you dancing in it. You will be the loveliest girl at any ball."

Chiara caught a quick glimpse of herself in the long mirror. Her dark hair fell over the ruffles of lace at the neckline and her eyes shone a vivid blue, echoed by the sash at her waist.

Then, as she turned back to Elizabeth and Madame Winterson, the skirts drifted around her legs like soft white mist and she suddenly wanted to dance and would have taken a few steps, if the shop had not been so small.

But then she remembered her Papa.

"I am still in mourning," she said. "It will be ages before I can go dancing again. I cannot have a lovely dress like this."

Both her friend and Madame Winterson tried hard to persuade her, but Chiara would not agree to take it.

"It's perfect," she sighed, "But I cannot – not now."

She ran back into the changing room and took off the white dress, putting her own frock, which she had worn at school, back on.

And then she left the shop and walked home with Elizabeth, as the afternoon sky was beginning to turn red with winter sunset.

"Everything will be all right," Elizabeth said and slid her arm through Chiara's.

Chiara nodded, but all her thoughts were far away,

back at Rensham Hall, a few days after her Papa's death.

All through the dark days following the death of her husband, Lady Fairfax had stayed in her bedroom with the door locked.

Chiara knocked many times and called out to her Mama, but only her maid, Margaret, was allowed to go inside.

"Her Ladyship is so distressed, Lady Chiara. She needs plenty of sleep and rest. She will see you when she is feeling better," Margaret said, when she found Chiara waiting outside the bedroom door.

It was agony for Chiara not be able to go in and comfort her Mama and be soothed in turn.

At the same time she could not get out of her mind the feeling that, if she had not come home from school on that day and her Papa not come hurrying to greet her, he might not have died.

Did her Mama blame her for what had happened, and was that why she would not speak to her?

When Lady Fairfax finally emerged from her room on Christmas Day and came down to breakfast, she looked pale and wan and had dark circles under her eyes.

Chiara ran to hug her before she could sit down.

"Mama, I am so glad to see you. I have been so worried about you."

Lady Fairfax pushed her gently away.

"I am fine, darling. It's just – I have had such a terrible shock. But I am feeling better now and I could not bear to think of you spending Christmas Day alone. We must be together and struggle through as best we can."

She sat down in her place and then began to pick at some toast and marmalade. Chiara thought that her heart might burst, if she did not speak the thoughts that had been tormenting her.

"Mama, you are not angry with me, are you?" she asked, when she could wait no longer.

Lady Fairfax sipped her coffee.

"Why should I be angry with you?" she asked in a tired voice.

Stumbling over her words, Chiara spoke of her fear that she might have been responsible for her Papa's heart attack. It was so painful to do this that she found herself crying uncontrollably.

Lady Fairfax stood up and came around the table to stroke her daughter's hair.

"Darling, you must absolutely forget such a foolish idea. Your dear Papa had been very ill for some time. We did not tell you because we knew you would be upset."

It was such a relief to hear those words, spoken so gently by her Mama, but then Chiara simply could not stop crying. Her whole body was shaking with violent sobs.

After a moment, she heard her mother say,

"My darling, I know how sad you are, but we have to get through today, when we will both be missing your Papa so terribly. And then – there is the funeral."

It had been arranged that Lord Fairfax would be buried before the New Year.

Lady Fairfax took Chiara's hand and gazed at her solemnly.

"Once the funeral is over, my darling, I think it would be a good idea if you went away for a little while."

"But – why, Mama? I want to stay here and look after you," Chiara exclaimed.

"No, my darling. We will end up just making each other even more upset. You must go and be with someone of your own age, who will cheer you up and help you to look forward to the future. That will be much better for you than being here brooding over what has happened."

Chiara felt her heart freezing like an icy stone as she heard this. How could she bear to go away?

But she could see that her mother was still full of grief and pain and had no strength to comfort her daughter. So she stopped crying.

Somehow Chiara got through both the long empty Christmas Day and the painful ritual of the funeral a few days later with perfect composure.

Then she had come here to Ely to be with her best friend, Elizabeth.

They were almost home now and were walking up the steep cobbled street that led to Elizabeth's house.

Suddenly Chiara heard the wild strange creaking noise that she had heard that morning, as she walked out over the Fens.

Above their heads, five swans were flying, their white feathers glowing pink in the light of the setting sun.

Chiara felt a glow of joy as she watched them.

Her stay here in Ely had already brought her some moments of happiness and maybe Elizabeth was right after all and perhaps everything would turn out well.

She squeezed her friend's arm.

"Shall we toast muffins again, when we get in?" she suggested.

"How delicious! I think we should. And thank you so much, Chiara, for helping me to choose such a lovely dress."

The swans had flown past now and were gone, but a little bit of the joyful feeling stayed with Chiara, as the two girls climbed up the front steps and went in through the blue door for tea.

CHAPTER THREE

"Chiara, the postman has brought a letter for you."

Elizabeth came running into the parlour with an envelope in her hand.

Chiara was attaching some pretty striped feathers to a little brown velvet hat that matched Elizabeth's new coat.

Outside the parlour windows, the bare branches of the trees were tossing about in the strong wind that often blew in across the Fens.

But the sun was shining on this bright February day and Chiara knew that spring would be coming soon.

"The postmark is Norfolk," Elizabeth said, as she handed Chiara the envelope.

"It will be from Mama."

Lady Fairfax had written a short note to her every week of the month that she had been away, sending her love and hoping that Chiara was enjoying herself in Ely.

As she unfolded the letter, Chiara was expecting to read a similar message to those her mother had already sent and she ran her eyes over the familiar elegant handwriting.

"*My darling daughter,* she read,

I hope that this letter finds you well and happy. I understand that you have been a great help to Elizabeth, as her Mama wrote to me last week and told me how hard you have been working to help her get ready for her wedding and what a joy it is to have you to stay with them.

As soon as I read her words, I realised how much I have missed my lovely daughter all through these sad and painful weeks.

It was very hard to send you away, but I knew that I would not be good company for you, my darling, and I so wanted you to have fun and not to dwell upon the sadness that hangs over our home.

I should love to have you home again, Chiara, if you can bear to leave the endless excitement of Elizabeth's engagement.

I am feeling very much better and people have been so very kind and thoughtful – not a day goes past without many callers coming to Rensham Hall. I have not yet received any of them, but I am quite inundated with their calling cards.

The time has come, I think, for me to face the world again. Don't you think it would be a good idea if we gave some dinner parties for these kind people?

And of course, I will need my lovely daughter at my side if I am going to start entertaining once more."

Chiara read no further, for her head was spinning with shock. Her Mama wanted her to go home!

She had been at Ely now for almost a month and she had become quite used to spending each and every day in Elizabeth's company, shopping and sewing, taking tea and going for long walks.

The Dean and his wife had treated her so kindly, almost as if she was a second daughter to them.

"What is it?" Elizabeth asked.

"Mama wants me to go back to Rensham Hall."

Elizabeth bit her lip.

"I am glad, but I shall miss you quite dreadfully."

"I do wish you could come with me," Chiara said, thinking how much fun it would be if the two of them were both able to attend the dinner parties her Mama mentioned.

"I really cannot." Elizabeth shook her head. "Not when I have so much to do before the wedding, but Chiara, – will you be my bridesmaid? Promise?"

"Of course!" Chiara said and gave her friend a hug.

*

The next day, as Chiara climbed into the chaise to begin her journey to Norfolk, Elizabeth pressed a brown paper parcel into her hands.

"Thank you for everything," she said. "Papa told me to choose a special present for you and this is it. Don't open it until you get home, will you?"

And then the chaise was soon rattling away over the cobblestones and Chiara turned back to wave at her friend, who stood on the steps as she had done on that first day, only now there were no black clouds in the sky and the spring sun was shining down on her glowing red hair.

This time, as she travelled up the drive to her home, Chiara did not look up at Rensham Hall. She could not bear to remember the last time she had arrived here.

When her mother came running down the stairs of Rensham Hall to greet her, Chiara's heart stopped beating for a moment. What if her Mama should trip on the stairs and fall at Chiara's feet, just like her father had done.

But Lady Fairfax did not stumble, she descended the staircase swiftly and gracefully, looking tall and elegant in a black mourning gown.

She was rather thinner than Chiara remembered and her face was very pale, but she seemed to have recovered much of her spirit.

"Oh, my darling! It's so good to see you," she said and flung her arms around Chiara. "Now you are here we can start to live again!"

"You look beautiful, Mama," Chiara sighed, gazing into Lady Fairfax's brown eyes and seeing that they were glowing with vitality once again.

"So do you, my Chiara. Why, the Fenland air must agree with you, you have such lovely roses in your cheeks. And you seem, I don't know, quite grown up!"

Chiara felt suddenly shy.

She had been only been away for a month, but she felt as if she had not seen her Mama for a very long time.

And she *did* feel grown up, after spending so much time with Elizabeth and planning for the wedding. Her days of being a carefree schoolgirl were now long past.

"But darling, just look at all these."

Lady Fairfax pointed to the silver tray that lay on the hall table, which was piled high with cards.

"Half of these people I don't even know," Lady Fairfax continued, picking up a handful of the cards. "Mr. Hunter? Who is he? I don't remember your Papa having an acquaintance of that name and here is a Lord Darley – I have certainly never met this person."

"It's very kind of everybody to call and offer their condolences, Mama."

"Indeed it is and we must repay that kindness. Now you are home, we must give dinner parties. First we must invite close friends and neighbours. Then we should extend our hospitality to some of these others we don't know. It might be fun to make some new acquaintances."

She turned to Chiara with a bright smile.

"I am quite looking forward to a little excitement," she said. "But now, my darling, you must go up to your room and settle yourself in."

But Lady Fairfax's social schedule did not work out quite as she had planned, as the first visitors to Rensham Hall were neither neighbours nor friends.

After breakfast the morning after her return home, Chiara took herself to the stables with a handful of sugar lumps for her old white pony, Erebus.

But before she could pass under the arch of the clock tower, which led into the stable yard, she heard the clatter of hooves behind her and turned, expecting to see one of the grooms bringing a pair of horses back from their morning exercise.

But the two handsome gentlemen who rode towards her on sleek thoroughbreds were complete strangers.

"It's her! Isn't it?" she heard the younger of the two say in a loud whisper. He had curly black hair and a round cheerful face.

"I hardly think so," the other gentleman replied. He was taller with a long tanned face and short brown hair that was turning grey at the sides.

The younger man put his hand up to his mouth and spoke behind it, but Chiara still heard him say,

"It has to be, she's pretty enough and look at her dark hair! Did they not say that Lady Fairfax came from Italy before she married?"

"Look again, my Lord," the other man whispered. "She's far too young to be a widow. This one is hardly out of school."

And then he smiled and raised his hat to Chiara.

"Good morning!" he called across to her. "Forgive us, we were not expecting to see a young lady out so bright and early. Mervyn Hunter at your service."

His teeth looked very white in his tanned face and his eyes were pale and sharp under his thin brows.

Chiara felt herself blushing. Before she could say anything, the younger man spoke,

"Lord Thomas Darley! Delighted to meet you," he said, sweeping his hat from his head. "We have been staying with Lord and Lady Duckett for the shooting."

"Good morning, my Lord," Chiara replied. "I hope your stay has been enjoyable."

"Absolutely!" Lord Darley said. "We've had great sport and now the season is over we thought we would stay on a while and have some gallops over your wonderful flat countryside."

He slapped his big brown horse on the shoulder and it tossed its head as if it was impatient to be off.

"But who are you?" he continued. "We have come past Rensham Hall several times to pay our respects to her Ladyship, but she never seems to be at home."

"I am her daughter. My name is Chiara."

"Oh, how very charming!" Lord Darley gave a little bow. "An Italian name, isn't it?"

"Yes."

Chiara felt rather uncomfortable as she stood by the archway, looking up at the two gentlemen. They seemed a long way above her as they sat on their tall thoroughbreds gazing down at her.

She did not know what she should do.

It seemed impolite not to invite them into The Hall for some refreshment, yet she was not sure how her Mama might feel about that.

Mervyn Hunter must have noticed that she was ill at ease, as he swung out of the saddle and dismounted.

"Do give our condolences to your dear mother," he said, pulling a calling card from out of his pocket. "Such a tragedy to lose her husband in that way."

Chiara wanted to back away from him, as he was standing very close, his pale eyes fixed on hers.

"Come on, Mervyn," Lord Darley urged, as his tall horse spun round. "Moonraker needs to stretch his legs."

Then to Chiara's relief, Mervyn Hunter leapt onto his mount and the two of them cantered away, their horses' hooves throwing up the gravel from the drive.

She made her way into the stable yard and found Erebus's white head peering over one of the stable doors.

She gave him his sugar and he pushed at her hand with his velvet nose, rolling his soft brown eyes, as if to tell her that he was pleased she had come back.

"He's missed you, Lady Chiara," a lilting Norfolk voice spoke. It was Jonah, the young groom who looked after Erebus. "Will you be ridin' out this mornin'?"

"Oh, I should love to, Jonah. But I must go in and tell Mama that we have had visitors."

Jonah looked at her, his blue eyes anxious under his thatch of thick fair hair.

"Those two, my Lady, they come a-ridin' by almost every day. What be they after?"

"They are staying with our friends, Lord and Lady Duckett," Chiara explained, "and they wished to pay their respects to Mama."

"Then why be they always a-snoopin' around the stable yard?" Jonah asked. "They've no business here and I've offered to put up their horses for 'em, but they always tell me they have just come to leave their cards and will be gone. So what do they mean by lookin' about the place?"

"I don't know, Jonah. Perhaps they like to see the horses."

Jonah shook his head.

"Neither of 'em cares one little bit for horseflesh,"

he said, "as they thinks nothin' of ridin' their beasts into the ground, just for the sake of speed."

"Well – don't you worry," Chiara said. "I will tell Mama about them and I am sure all will be well."

Jonah was clearly worried by the behaviour of these two gentlemen and Chiara too felt a little uneasy when she recalled the way that Mervyn Hunter had looked at her.

His lean face was indeed handsome enough, but he had stared at her so intently that she did not feel quite comfortable under his cold gaze.

She wished that her Papa was still alive as he would know exactly how to handle the situation, but he was not and no amount of wishing would bring him back.

Chiara promised Jonah that she would ride the next day and, with a swift kiss for Erebus on his soft nose, she ran back to The Hall.

"So that is a mystery solved!" Lady Fairfax cried, when Chiara told her about the visitors. "Those two very handsome gentlemen I spied from the window are Lord Darley and Mr. Hunter, who have left their cards for us."

"Mama – did you see them?"

"I did indeed," Lady Fairfax replied and a pretty dimple appeared in her cheek as she smiled. "I was about to come out and meet them, but then I saw that you were there first and I did not want to spoil your fun!"

"Oh, Mama! You should have come."

"Not at all, my darling. The tall distinguished one Lord Darley, I presume, has quite fallen for you, I think – I saw him leap from the saddle to speak to you."

Chiara explained that this was Mr. Hunter and that his companion was in fact Lord Darley.

"Is that so?" Lady Fairfax's eyes were now shining. "Well, my darling, then it's Mr. Hunter who is smitten with you and what a striking man! Though Lord Darley is very good-looking too. I am going straight to my writing desk to compose an invitation to dinner. Let's have Lord and Lady Duckett and their very handsome guests to dine with us at the first possible opportunity."

Chiara could not remember seeing her Mama so excited and happy before and she found herself wondering if sometimes she had found being married to a man much older than herself a little dull, even though she loved him very much.

At the same time the thought was a rather upsetting one and Chiara pushed it into the back of her mind as she went up to her bedroom to wash and tidy her hair.

The first thing she noticed, as she entered the room, was a brown paper parcel lying on the sofa.

"Elizabeth's present! How could I have forgotten it?"

Somehow in the excitement of arriving at Rensham Hall last night, it had completely slipped Chiara's mind. Her maid must have found the parcel among her things and laid it on the sofa for her to open.

She picked it up and weighed it in her hands. It felt light and soft. When she tore open the brown paper, Chiara caught her breath in delight. Inside was the white dress with the blue sash she had tried on in the shop in Ely.

Elizabeth must have gone back and bought it for her. Tears of joy and gratitude sprang into Chiara's eyes.

'It's the loveliest dress ever,' she sighed to herself. 'Now all I need is a ball to go to!'

And then she tenderly folded the cloudy white silk, touching the filmy lace of the neckline and the sleeves and took it to hang up in her wardrobe.

A note had come with the parcel and she picked it up to read,

"Dearest Chiara,

I will never forget how lovely you looked when you tried this dress in that shop – so here it is! I told Papa about it and he completely agreed that you should have it. Which is quite something from dear Papa, who normally does not bother about things like that.

I wanted you to have the dress as a thank you for everything you have done whilst you stayed with us. You really are the kindest friend in the whole world.

I just know that very soon you are going to meet someone absolutely perfect and fall in love – and when that does happen you will need to look your best, so you must promise me you will wear the dress and not just hang it up!

And Chiara, you must let me know the minute your special beau comes along. Promise.

All my best love,

Elizabeth."

Chiara could not help smiling. She *was* glad to be home, but it would have been wonderful to have Elizabeth with her to talk to and what would her friend have made of the two gentlemen she had encountered that morning?

She went to her writing desk to pen a 'thank you' note and found herself describing them – Lord Darley with his wide smile and curly hair and the handsome Mervyn Hunter, who had gazed at her so intently.

Elizabeth would enjoy reading about them, she was sure.

*

Over the coming days Chiara found that Mervyn. Hunter kept coming into her mind. Why had he stared at her in that way? Was it true that he was 'smitten with her', as her Mama seemed to think?

A date had been fixed for Lord and Lady Duckett

and their two gentlemen guests to come to luncheon and every time Chiara thought of seeing Mervyn Hunter again, a little shiver of anticipation passed through her body.

It was almost a pleasant sensation, but it made her feel uneasy too, as if she was just a little afraid.

On the morning of the luncheon, a letter came for Chiara with an Ely postmark. It was from Elizabeth.

Oh, Chiara – I think this might be it! Mr. Hunter might be the one. You say he is very handsome and that he gazed at you for a very long time. Have you been thinking about him? And does he make you feel slightly weak at the knees? If you do feel like that, Chiara, it could be love!

Chiara did not know what to think. It was true that she could not get Mervyn Hunter out of her mind.

She had not seen him for several days and perhaps she had been mistaken about him, maybe there was nothing odd at all about the way he had stared at her and he had just been admiring her.

Arthur had certainly been unable to take his eyes off Elizabeth whenever she had seen them together.

She took the white dress out of the wardrobe and held it against herself. Should she wear it? It would be lovely to feel the soft silk rustling around her ankles and the delicate lace caressing her neck and arms.

But it was an evening gown and not really suitable for luncheon.

As she sat in the drawing room later that afternoon, she was very glad indeed that she had not worn the white dress, but had stuck to one of her sensible long-sleeved, dark gowns.

The luncheon party had gone very well. Lord and Lady Duckett were old family friends and Lord Duckett had attended the same school as Chiara's Papa.

They were both delighted to see that Lady Fairfax was recovering from her bereavement and Lord Duckett's lined face was wreathed in smiles as he proposed a toast to 'happier days at Rensham Hall.'

Lady Duckett was fulsome in her praise of the food and wine.

"How well you are managing, my dear, without your husband. What a resourceful woman you are," she kept saying.

She ate and drank a good deal and then, as the meal progressed, Lady Duckett became rather quiet and several times Chiara thought that she was about to doze off.

It was young Lord Darley who had much to say, sat opposite Chiara's Mama and made several toasts to her.

He said he absolutely agreed with Lady Duckett. Lady Fairfax was a remarkable hostess to have produced such a delicious luncheon.

And how flattering those dark clothes of mourning were to a woman of her striking complexion, he added.

Mervyn Hunter, who sat opposite Chiara, said very little, but she knew that he was watching her, as every time she looked up from her plate, her eyes met his.

'Elizabeth and Mama must indeed be right,' she thought, 'he *does* like me!'

She looked up once again and this time she smiled at him.

Mervyn Hunter raised his brows and sat back in his chair. His thin lips curled as he returned her smile, but his grey eyes remained quite cold.

Chiara's cheeks felt hot and she knew that she must have been blushing. She wished now she had not smiled.

She dropped her gaze to her plate and tried to keep

it fixed there. She thought of Arthur and the way that his expression was gentle and warm whenever he looked at Elizabeth. There was nothing at all gentle about the way Mervyn Hunter smiled at her.

"I would like to propose a toast!" he was saying now in his dry sardonic voice. "To a blossoming young lady who promises to be every bit as pretty as her lovely Mama!"

He raised his glass and now his eyes were narrowed so that Chiara thought he was like a cat about to pounce on a bird.

"Oh, no, really – please don't – " she began, before she could stop herself.

But Lord Darley then gave a little cheer and raised his glass too and then everyone stood up to toast her.

The rest of the meal was agony for Chiara.

Mervyn Hunter now had a permanent smile on his lean face.

She managed not to look at him and then suddenly she felt something touch her foot. She jumped and could not help but raise her eyes to him and now Mervyn Hunter was laughing at her.

He reached out again, pressing her toes with his booted foot and Chiara shuddered and, in spite of herself, rose from table.

"What is it, darling?" her Mama asked and then to Chiara's great relief, she suggested that it might be time to retire to the drawing room.

"Let's make ourselves a little more comfortable, ladies," she said. "I am sure that the gentlemen will enjoy a cigar or two in the smoking room."

Lady Duckett settled down for a snooze, propped against the sofa cushions and Lady Fairfax turned to her daughter.

For a moment, Chiara thought she was going to ask about what had happened at table and that she would be able to tell her mother about Mervyn Hunter's behaviour.

But Lady Fairfax was oblivious of her distress.

"Chiara – Lord Darley has been to Italy – several times! Isn't that marvellous? He says he almost wishes he was an Italian himself. We have so much in common, I cannot quite believe it!"

Her Mama's face was glowing with happiness and Chiara could not bear to interrupt and spoil her pleasure.

It was not long before the door opened and the drawing room was suddenly filled with men's loud voices and the strong scent of cigar smoke.

Chiara's heart suddenly jumped as Mervyn Hunter approached her and drew up a chair so that he was sitting facing her.

"You are a very modest little thing, aren't you?" he said, his voice very quiet, so that no one else could hear. "Why so shy?"

Chiara turned to her Mama, but Lady Fairfax was standing in front of the fireplace her hand in Lord Darley's, laughing and talking.

Mervyn Hunter leaned forward, his face as close to hers as it had been on the day they first met. She tried to move back, but she was trapped in her chair and there was no escape.

His cold grey eyes were fixed upon hers and Chiara could not look away.

CHAPTER FOUR

"Why won't you look at me?" Mervyn Hunter said so softly that no one else in the room could hear him. "A short while ago at luncheon you were all smiles and now you will not even meet my eyes."

Chiara longed to jump up from her chair and run out of the drawing room, but he was leaning so close to her that, if she stood up, she would almost be in his arms.

"What have I done?" he asked, staring intently at her with his pale grey eyes. "Have I said something to upset you?"

"No."

Chiara shook her head.

"Aha!" he smiled. "I've got it! It was our little game under the table, wasn't it?"

She could not help giving an involuntary shiver, as she remembered his heavy foot pressing against hers.

"But why should you be so upset? I thought you might find it amusing," he carried on.

His voice was very soft, but the expression in his eyes was cold as he watched Chiara.

"I did not," she said, the words coming out more sharply than she intended and then to her great relief, he moved back from her a little.

"My sincere apologies," he said. "I did not mean to cause offence. It was just a little fun."

"Chiara, darling!" Lady Fairfax called across the drawing room. She was now sitting on the sofa with Lord Darley. "Will you ring for the card table to be brought in? We should like to play."

"Of course, Mama."

Now everybody was looking at her and she found it easier to stand up and edge past Mervyn Hunter.

He would not try to touch her or push her back into her chair in full view of everybody.

She went over to the marble fireplace and tugged on the long velvet bell-pull that hung there,

And then, instead of returning to her chair, she went to stand by the sofa, where her Mama was sitting with Lord Darley.

Two parlourmaids came hurrying in and put up the little green baize card table in the middle of the room.

"Will you play with us too, Chiara?" Lord Darley looked up at her.

His eyes were bright with enthusiasm and Chiara thought, as she had when she first saw him in the stable yard, that he seemed a very cheerful person.

"I would love to," she answered, breathing a sigh of relief.

"No, no!" Lord Duckett ambled over, his kindly red face wreathed in white whiskers. "The young lady is just becoming acquainted with Mr. Hunter and we should not interrupt their *tête-à-tête*!"

One of the parlourmaids pulled up a chair to the card table and Lord Duckett sat down heavily upon it and planted his gnarled hands on the green baize.

"Come along, Maud!" he called in a loud voice to his wife. "Rouse yourself, my dear. You are needed for whist."

Lady Duckett gave a little jump and sat up straight. Then she rose unsteadily and came to join her husband.

Mervyn Hunter made his way to Chiara's side, a smile on his thin lips.

"Saved!" he murmured to her and then, moving his lips close to her ear, he added, "I cannot think of anything more tedious on a lovely spring afternoon than to be stuck at a card table."

To her horror, she felt him take hold of her hand and press it with his.

Lord Darley was now leading her Mama to the card table and, as soon as they sat down, Lord Duckett began to deal the cards.

"Oh, what luck!" Mervyn Hunter murmured. "The sofa has become vacant. Let's take full advantage of its comfort and seclusion."

Chiara pulled her hand out of his and shook her head.

"What's wrong now?" he asked. "I cannot believe that you would rather watch a game of cards than enjoy a peaceful conversation with a gentleman who admires you as much as I do – "

Before Chiara could reply, her Mama turned to her and asked,

"Are you all right, my dear? You look very pale."

"I am not feeling very well," Chiara replied.

She was about to ask if she might go to her room, but Mervyn Hunter, still close beside her, interrupted.

"Fresh air, I think, is called for," he said. "May I have the pleasure of escorting you for a short walk on the terrace, Lady Chiara?"

"Mr. Hunter, what a kind thought!" Lady Fairfax nodded her approval. "By all means, go out, both of you, and enjoy the sunshine. Chiara's spirits will soon revive."

"No – I – really don't want to," Chiara stammered.

"A walk will do you good, darling. You love to be out of doors." Lady Fairfax said, looking a little surprised.

Mervyn Hunter held out his arm and Chiara had no choice but to place her hand on it and follow him out of Rensham Hall and onto the terrace that ran along the house.

"Well!" he exclaimed, as he tucked Chiara's hand under his arm, trapping it there with his elbow. "This is very nice, isn't it? Just the two of us, alone at last."

She did not reply, but looked away from him and out over the Park, wishing that he would not keep gazing at her so intently.

"I see I am still out of favour," he began, after they had walked a few more yards. "But I am only trying to please you. Surely, if you are feeling unwell, a short walk in the company of a kind and handsome gentleman should be just the thing?"

Chiara turned to face him.

"I should like to go inside now," she said.

He sighed.

"You are so cold to me, Lady Chiara."

"I should like to go in," she repeated, striving to keep her voice level. "I don't wish to walk with you."

"Ah, perhaps 'cold' is not quite strong enough. I might almost say that you are rude, my Lady. Perhaps you took a little too much wine with your luncheon and that is what is causing this strange mood!"

"I did not!" Chiara snapped. "You were watching me almost all the time, you must have seen that I only took a few sips."

"Oh, that's much better!" He stopped. "Now you are looking me in the eye and showing me a little spirit and I like it very much."

He caught Chiara's wrists in his hands and spun her around to face him.

"How lovely you are, Chiara, even when you are scowling at me."

"Let me go!"

He was very strong and, although Chiara tried with all her strength to free her hands, she could not.

"I will, when I am ready," he said. "But first of all, since I have spent so long trying to please you, I am going to insist that I have a little something in return – "

He was interrupted by a loud rapping noise on the glass of one of the windows nearby.

Mervyn Hunter swore under his breath and turned his back to the window, but still keeping a tight hold on Chiara's wrists.

She then heard the squeak of the casement window opening and Lord Duckett's voice calling to them.

"I say, Mr. Hunter! Disaster. Maud has nodded off over her hand of cards! Our game is ruined. Would you come and partner me, sir? I need your superlative talents at the card table or I am sure to lose."

The old man's whiskered face peered anxiously out of the open window, as he added,

"If the young lady has no objection? Perhaps she has walked for long enough?"

Mervyn Hunter's white teeth flashed in a smile, as he called over his shoulder,

"Absolutely, Lord Duckett! Lady Chiara is a little under the weather and does not wish to walk any further. I shall be with you in an instant."

The window squeaked shut again.

"Ha – we were right outside the drawing room. But I don't think that the old man saw a thing."

He drew Chiara along the terrace so that they were out of view of the drawing room window.

Chiara's heart was beating painfully fast. What did he mean, when he said that he wanted to take something from her?

"You must go," she urged him as politely as she could manage, "they are waiting for you."

"Let them."

"Please, *just go!*"

Chiara twisted her arms inside his grip, but he did not budge.

"You don't realise how much I care for you, do you?" he was saying. "Do you seriously think that I mean you harm?"

"Let go of me, please!"

"For, Chiara, this little thing that I am going to claim in recompense for all the attention I have offered you – why – had you not thought it might be something nice?"

Before Chiara could think what he meant or how she should reply to it, he had bent his head and brushed his mouth against hers.

His lips were hot and the touch of them sent a shock through her whole body. Her legs shook and she almost fell against him.

"See. Was that so bad?" his pale eyes had a strange light in them as they looked into hers. "Another one? No, I think I will make you wait for it."

And then he did let her go and she watched him walk away from her along the terrace.

She was trembling so much that she had to sit down on one of the little stone garden seats.

*

"Remarkable creatures!"

King Edward VII's manicured hand rested for a moment on the silky head of one of the tall white Borzoi hounds that Count Dimitrov had given him that morning, when he arrived at Sandringham to begin his visit.

"Alas, we have no wolves at Sandringham for them to chase!"

Arkady bowed, politely.

"I am sure that they will not mind, sir, to leave the dangers of that most perilous sport behind them."

"How graceful they are," the Queen remarked. "An ornament to any room they inhabit. I should think they would make excellent pets. Will you have another cup of coffee, Count Dimitrov?"

"Thank you, ma'am, but I am more than replete after your delicious luncheon."

In fact, Arkady was feeling uncomfortably full. So many rich courses had been brought to the long table in the dining room and he had eaten far too much. He shifted his position on the small uncomfortable gilt chair where he sat.

"I cannot help but think, Count, that you are rather like a Borzoi yourself!" the Queen was saying, a Regal smile on her face. "You are so tall and you have the same air of strength and grace that they have."

Arkady laughed.

"Thank you, ma'am. An unusual compliment!"

"We really do want you to enjoy your stay here at Sandringham," the Queen continued. "This is one of our favourite residences and you must feel quite at home here."

Arkady bowed again and now the King was asking him how he liked Norfolk.

"I have seen only glimpses on my journey here," he replied, "but the flat landscape reminds me of my country estate in Russia. I should like to know more about it."

The King looked pleased and he then told Arkady to wander wherever he liked in the gardens and grounds around the house.

But flowerbeds and prettily clipped bushes were not what Arkady really cared for that afternoon. He seemed to have been cooped up indoors for so many weeks now and he longed to roam free.

He could have gone to the stables and asked for a horse or even a chaise, so that he could go further afield, and he was about to do so, when something caught his eye.

An old bicycle was leaning up against the wall of the garden.

Arkady had never ridden a bicycle before and he wondered what it would be like.

Why should he not give it a try? He went over and took hold of the handlebars, noticing that someone had tied a rolled-up woollen coat onto the back of the bicycle.

Arkady wheeled the bicycle onto the smooth grass of the lawn, straddled it and launched himself forward.

"Hey!" a voice cried.

Arkady looked around to see who had spoken, and in the next moment found himself lying flat on the grass, the bicycle on top of him.

"What do you think you're doin'?" a young lad in work clothes was running up to him. "Oh, excuse me, sir."

The lad blushed a fiery red and took his cap off.

"I am Count Dimitrov," Arkady said, standing and brushing a few dead leaves from his trousers, "and this I presume is your bicycle?"

"Yes it is, um – Count Dimitrov." The young man asked, looking anxiously at Arkady. "Are you hurt, sir?"

"Only in my pride. And who are you?"

"Jeremy, sir, Jeremy Jones. I work in the gardens, here."

"So, how does one master this thing?"

Arkady picked up the bicycle from the grass and stood it on its wheels.

"Well, it's easy once you know how!" Jeremy said and then he added, politely, "although I don't know how many times I fell off when I was learnin'."

"Show me how to do it!" Arkady requested.

Jeremy took the bicycle and demonstrated how to mount it and then how to turn the pedals and make it go forward.

Arkady tried again, but, although his balance was somewhat better this time, he could not seem to get the bicycle moving very well.

"It's difficult on the grass," Jeremy said, "because the ground is damp and it's slowin' the wheels down. It's easier on the road."

"Then let's go there!"

"If you don't mind me sayin', sir, the grass is softer to fall on!"

But Arkady was already wheeling the boy's bicycle towards the drive.

Jeremy ran after him.

"Sir. I would come with you, but I have duties in the garden."

"Of course! Go back to work. I will return your bicycle when I have mastered the art of riding it."

The young lad looked doubtful, but then the Head Gardener was approaching, pushing a wheelbarrow full of young plants and he knew that he must take them and start digging them into the flowerbeds.

So he said nothing as Arkady mounted the bicycle again and wobbled precariously away.

It was hard going at first and Arkady kept having to put one or other of his feet to the ground to keep upright, which meant that his progress along the narrow country lanes was very slow.

But gradually he found that he could keep his feet on the pedals for one or two complete revolutions and then he realised that the faster he went, the easier it was to keep his balance.

Suddenly the bicycle began to pick up speed as the lane took a gentle slope downwards. Arkady took his feet off the pedals and found himself flying forwards, his hair blowing back in the wind.

He had no idea where he was going, but ahead of him in the distance, he could see the sun shining on a wide expanse of blue water, which must be the sea.

*

"Lady Chiara!" Jonah dropped the bundle of hay he was carrying and peered over the door into Erebus's stable. "Whatever be wrong?"

He had caught her unawares and Chiara buried her face in Erebus's long white mane to hide the fact that she had been crying.

"It's nothing, really, I am just a little upset."

But Jonah continued,

"It isn't that Mr. Hunter, is it? I know he's here, as I had to take his horse from him when he arrived. I saw him speakin' to you when he was here before."

Chiara stayed silent.

She did not know what to say. She could not tell Jonah that Mervyn Hunter had kissed her and left her full of a strange excitement that was so strong it frightened her.

"A nervous creature the poor beast is, too!" Jonah said. "No gentleman should ride a fine thoroughbred horse like that so hard. Drenched in sweat, it was, when he gave the reins to me."

"Poor thing. But I am sure you have taken good care of it, Jonah."

"Indeed. I put him in the little paddock to relax and enjoy the sun. But will you not ride today, my Lady?"

She looked down at her silk skirts.

"I cannot, Jonah."

Her sensible woollen riding habit was hanging in her wardrobe and she did not want to go back to the house to change, in case she encountered Mervyn Hunter again.

"That's a pity, as it's a perfect afternoon for a ride," Jonah said and, as Erebus nudged Chiara with his nose, he added, "see! He agrees with me."

"I *will* ride!" Chiara cried. "Saddle him for me!"

The sunshine was warmer than usual on this spring afternoon and it would not matter at all that she was only wearing a thin dress.

It would be Heaven to feel the soft wind in her hair, blowing away all the unpleasantness of luncheon and she did not intend to go far. Just a quick turn around the Park.

Erebus was a fine spirited creature with hot Arabian blood running in his veins and he was overjoyed to feel Chiara's light weight on his back again. He knew that she would let him gallop, instead of trotting sedately along the roads, as he did for his daily exercise with the groom.

He tossed his head, tugging hard at his reins and he then danced over the gravel with little prancing steps in his impatience to be speeding across the Park.

"Steady!" Chiara told him, for it had been many weeks since she had ridden and she had almost forgotten what is was like to sit on an eager lively horse.

As soon as they left the drive and Erebus felt the soft springy turf of the Park under his feet, he broke into a swift bounding canter.

Chiara's hair was soon tumbling down around her shoulders and she felt the cool breeze on her face as they flew forward towards a copse of trees.

"Oh, this is so lovely!" she cried out and Erebus flicked his little white ears back at the sound of her voice.

Suddenly a cock pheasant ran out from the trees, flapping its wings wildly and then darted right in front of Erebus.

The pony jumped sideways and Chiara felt the reins slip through her fingers as he leapt into a gallop, heading for the main gates that led out of the Park onto the road.

*

Arkady had lost all sense of time.

He was having a glorious afternoon, now that he had finally mastered the difficult art of staying upright on the bicycle and he sped along deserted lanes that wound their way between green fields until he had lost all sense of direction.

He had absolutely no idea how to get back to the King's country house at Sandringham and he did not care.

He was free and he wanted to keep going on and on as fast as he could.

After a while, much to his annoyance, the lane that he was bicycling along grew narrow and overgrown and turned into a rutted cart track.

But still he did not feel like turning back, so he dismounted and walked on, wheeling the bicycle, until the track emerged among sandy hillocks with tall pine trees growing on them.

Arkady climbed to the top of one of the hillocks and caught his breath in astonishment.

Stretching out in front of him there was mile upon mile of glowing golden sands and beyond them, the silvery shimmer of water.

He had reached the sea.

He laid the bicycle down and sat beside it, gazing at the expanse of beauty that lay before him.

The wind blowing off the sea was cold and so he unrolled the old coat that was strapped onto the back of the bicycle and pushed his arms through the tattered sleeves.

The beach was deserted, except for a few seagulls and he sat for a long time, staring out to sea and thinking of his homeland, until the sky began to turn pink.

*

Erebus's hooves clattered as he raced along the open road and Chiara soon gave up her efforts to stop him, as her arms were aching and something in her heart longed to just let go and let him carry her wherever he liked.

Soon she realised that Erebus was heading for the beach and for the vast expanse of smooth sand where in the past they had shared so many wonderful gallops.

As they clambered down the dunes onto the beach, Erebus paused for a moment to catch his breath and then he was off again, his hooves drumming over the wet sand.

Chiara cried out for joy, as it was like flying to go so fast, with the wind whistling in her hair and tugging at her silk dress.

It was as if at any moment now they would be up and borne away into the glorious evening sky just beginning to show the first rosy tints of sun

Erebus ran and ran, until at last he began to tire and his legs began to falter.

"Come now, we must turn back," Chiara called out to him, patting his shoulder as he slowed to a walk.

A cold wind was now blowing off the sea and she shivered, because her dress was wet where salt water had splashed up from Erebus's hooves.

And then a different kind of chill struck her, as a tall ragged-looking, dark-haired stranger was walking now towards them across the sand.

"I thought there was no one here!" she whispered, feeling exposed and vulnerable in her thin dress as the odd figure drew nearer.

Who was he? And what reason did he have to be here in this lonely place?

Now he was quite close and looking up at her with a mysterious expression in his dark eyes.

"*Mademoiselle*," he now began in a deep voice. "I thought your little horse had wings and I was waiting for you both to fly away, but you have come down to earth!"

Chiara dug her heels into Erebus's sides urging him to move on, but he stood stock still, staring at the stranger.

The man remained where he was, a little smile on his face.

"Who – who are you?" she asked, looking at the ragged dirty coat he wore. "Surely you don't come from around here. You don't sound like a Norfolk man."

ıghed.

ɜ quite right. I am a visitor. And you, I
ʻɪ the sky?"

urse not – I have just come – to ride,"
difficulty, as her teeth were beginning
ɔld.

"In a silk dress? With your hair flying loose like an angel in a painting? And all alone? I think you are fooling with me. You are a Heavenly being just fallen to earth."

And then he shook his head.

"But no, you must be mortal after all – for you are shivering. Here!"

He pulled off his ragged coat and held it out to her and she was astonished to see that he wore an elegant grey morning coat and beautifully cut trousers underneath it.

"Please, I insist!" he said and tossed the coat up to her so that it fell around her shoulders.

"But – who *are* you?" she asked. "I cannot take your coat if I don't know who to return it to and you will be cold without it."

"It's not my coat," he replied, "and, just for today, I am nobody, lost in a strange land."

He threw back his head and laughed again.

"Go, quickly!" he shouted. "Back to your home in the sky!"

He clapped his hands so that Erebus was startled and shied away from him.

Chiara clutched the ragged coat around her with one hand and clung to the reins with the other.

Erebus was turning for home now and the stranger was leaving, running with long loping strides as he headed for the dunes at the top of the beach.

"Thank you!" she called, but he did not turn back.

CHAPTER FIVE

Chiara's heart now leapt with excitement as Erebus cantered swiftly back over the beach.

She could not get the dark-haired stranger's face out of her mind.

His high cheekbones and the fierce glow of his dark eyes seemed strangely familiar and yet she was certain that she had never met him before.

And the sound of his voice!

When she remembered his curious accent and the odd things he had said to her, her whole body rang with a sensation she had never felt before, as if she was a silver bell giving out a sweet high note.

The sun had fallen below the horizon and the sky was turning purple as they left the beach.

Chiara knew they might not get back to Rensham Hall before dark, but Erebus would have no trouble finding the way even though there was no moon.

The little pony kept a steady trot along the narrow country roads and Chiara slackened the reins and let him make his own pace.

She was very glad of the stranger's dusty old coat, as, now that the sun had set, the air was turning very cold.

Suddenly, Erebus's ears flicked back, as if he had heard something and he jumped forward, quickening his pace.

Chiara strained to catch the sound that had startled him and her heart quickened because she could hear men's voices shouting and a distant clatter of hooves on the road.

Riders were galloping along the road behind her.

"Go on, go on, as fast as you can," she whispered, leaning low over Erebus's white mane. "I don't want them to see me out riding in the dusk in my silk dress and this funny old coat."

But the little pony was tired from his long gallop on the beach and, although he tried valiantly to keep ahead, the noise of the shouting grew steadily nearer.

"Hello there! Lady Chiara? Where are you?"

A chill ran through Chiara's limbs, as she heard her name being called out. It was Mervyn Hunter's voice and it was he who was on her trail.

"We must take a short cut!" she cried.

She pulled the reins, turning Erebus's head so that he had to leap up the steep bank that bordered the road.

Now they were in the fields and ahead of them in the gloomy twilight, a bright light winked and Chiara knew that this must be coming from a window at Rensham Hall.

"We're almost there!" she called and dug her heels into the pony's sides.

He stumbled forward across the deep furrows of the ploughed field, pushing on as fast as he could, as the faint scent of home was drifting towards them and he wanted to be safely there as much as his Mistress.

For a moment Chiara thought she had outwitted her pursuers, but then a great shout went up from the road.

"I see her! Look, her white horse, there in the field!"

Then the thud of hooves came crashing over the muddy ground and Mervyn Hunter's thoroughbred raced up alongside Erebus.

"Whoa, there! Stop I say!" he shouted out and he reached down from his saddle and caught the reins out of Chiara's hands, tugging on them so hard that Erebus was dragged off balance and he staggered and fell to his knees.

Chiara was flung over his head and hit the ground so hard that all the breath was knocked from her body.

"I say. Is she all right?" Lord Darley cantered up, leaping down from the saddle to kneel beside Chiara.

"That brute threw her!" Mervyn Hunter exclaimed, throwing the reins at Erebus's head. "Get away! Be off with you!"

Erebus limped away across the furrows.

Chiara wanted to call out to him to come back and that he had done nothing wrong, but she was struggling to breath and could not speak.

"My poor sweetheart!" Mervyn Hunter leant down from the saddle. "Can you lift her up to me, Lord Darley?"

Chiara felt herself being lifted high in the air and then Mervyn Hunter's strong arms went round her, holding her in front of him as his tall horse bounded across the fields towards Rensham Hall.

Night was finally falling as they clattered under the echoing archway that led into the stable yard.

Lady Fairfax was standing in the yard, surrounded by servants carrying lanterns.

"Oh, my darling!" she cried out, her face pale in the flickering light. "Thank God they have found you!"

Chiara had recovered her breath, but his arms still held her in a vice-like grip, perched in front of him on his tall horse.

"Mama, I am so sorry. I did not mean to be out for so long. I intended just to ride around the Park – "

Jonah now came up to them leading Erebus, who had found his way back across the fields to the stable yard.

"Ah, ha, there is the culprit!" Mervyn Hunter said, holding Chiara so tightly that she felt the vibration of his deep voice against her.

"What happened?" Jonah's face was puzzled. "The little pony always brings you safely home."

Chiara was about to explain that Erebus had been doing exactly that, until Mervyn Hunter made him fall, but she was interrupted.

"God knows what might have happened if we had not been there!" he snapped. "The beast was completely out of control."

Lady Fairfax gave a little cry of horror and pressed her hands to her face in horror.

"My poor sweet daughter!" she muttered.

Lord Darley jumped down from his horse and came over.

"Lady Fairfax, please – don't be distressed. See – all is well. She has not been hurt."

He then took Chiara's hands and helped her to jump down from Mervyn Hunter's horse.

"Mama, I am really quite all right," she began, but Lady Fairfax was looking at her with alarm.

"What is this horrid thing?" she asked, touching the tattered coat Chiara was wearing.

"A gentleman gave me his coat, Mama."

"A *gentleman*?" Lady Fairfax shook her head in disbelief. "But this is just a dirty old rag!"

Chiara was about to explain about her encounter with the dark-haired man in the elegant morning suit, when Mervyn Hunter spoke again.

"Perhaps Lady Chiara has been paying a visit to the raggle-taggle gypsies!" he sneered, "she certainly managed to give us the slip for quite some time. Was by chance this 'gentleman' of the Romany people?"

"I – don't think so – " Chiara hesitated.

She could not place the dark-haired man's foreign accent she had liked so much, but she was quite certain that no Romany would have worn an immaculate morning suit.

"Promise me, my darling, that you will never go off like that again."

Lady Fairfax had overcome her repugnance for the dirty old coat and was taking Chiara in her arms to hug her.

"Not much chance of that," Mervyn Hunter piped up, watching as Jonah led Erebus to his stable. "The brute that threw her is quite lame."

"Oh, no!" Chiara cried. "My poor Erebus! It really was not his fault. If you had not pulled the reins so hard, and frightened him – "

"Chiara!" Lady Fairfax spoke up sharply. "You are being exceedingly ungrateful. These two gentlemen have been riding around the countryside in search of you and have stopped at nothing to make sure that you came safely home – and you have said not one word of thanks."

"Oh, there is no need!" Lord Darley exclaimed. "I am just so glad she is safe. And it was no trouble, really, we would have done anything to find you, Chiara."

Mervyn Hunter leapt down from the saddle.

"We searched high and low," he declared, "and the moment of finding you, Lady Chiara, was the sweetest of my life."

He took her hand and raised it to his lips, bowing as he did so.

Lady Fairfax was frowning at Chiara, reproving her for her bad manners and she knew that she must say some words of thanks.

"I am most – grateful," she managed. "It was very kind of you to make – such efforts on my behalf."

Then she could not help adding,

"But I am used to taking long rides round Rensham Hall and, although it was late and I had gone further than I meant to, I was perfectly safe."

Mervyn Hunter shook his head and reached out and fingered the sleeve of the old coat.

"Perhaps you are not the best judge of that, Lady Chiara," he said. "It's not wise for a young lady to ride off on her own and speak to any old stranger she meets."

Then he gave a little laugh.

"Hopefully the occasion will never arise – but if you do see this 'gentleman' again – you might advise him to visit to my tailor, as he is in dire need of a new coat!"

Chiara felt a rush of anger, but she gave a polite nod to Mervyn Hunter and turned her back on him, ready to walk back to Rensham Hall.

But he had not finished.

"Surely, Lady Chiara, this filthy old garment would best be left with your young groom until you are ready to visit the gypsy camp again!"

He called out to Jonah, who was feeding Erebus.

"Come here, boy!"

Chiara's face now grew hot. How dare he speak to Jonah like that and now he was lifting the coat from her shoulders and thrusting it at the groom like an old sack.

She wanted to take it back and keep it in her room to remind her of the dark-haired man on the beach, who had looked at her so mysteriously.

Her maid could have brushed all the dirt away, so that if ever she saw him again, she could give it back to him in a clean and respectable condition, more in keeping with his elegant grey suit.

But Jonah was taking the coat away to the harness room.

Lord Darley was whispering something to Lady Fairfax, who was nodding and looking pleased.

Mervyn Hunter took Chiara's hand and lifted it to his lips.

"It will not be long before we meet again," he said. "And I do hope that you will stay safely at home till then."

"Goodbye, Mr. Hunter."

Chiara took a step back.

"Every moment spent in your delightful company is pure pleasure," he continued in a low voice, as he released her hand.

At last Chiara was free to run across the stable yard, the evening air chill on her face and escape to the privacy of her bedroom.

*

"My dear Count Dimitrov!" the King's bearded face was alight with amusement. "What an adventurer you are! I did not take you for a bicyclist, I must say!"

Arkady sipped the glass of whisky he was enjoying before going into dinner. He had only just had time to change into his evening clothes, as it had taken him a good while to find his way back to Sandringham from the coast.

"The bicycle is a remarkable invention," he said. "Much faster and more efficient than a horse, if one sticks to the road."

The King laughed.

"I am only sorry that you had to resort to borrowing from one of the under-gardeners! If you could only have waited a little, we should have arranged for a brand new machine to be bought for you."

Arkady could not help smiling.

"Ah, sir – but I think the Fates wished otherwise!"

"Whatever do you mean, Count," the Queen looked at him in surprise. "You are sounding very mysterious – very Russian, in fact!"

"I chanced upon an angel today," he replied, "and I think if I had gone exploring at some other time, I would have missed that meeting."

"Now you are telling us a Russian Fairy tale!" the Queen responded with a regal smile.

"Not at all, ma'am. A wild and beautiful angel on a winged white horse flew down from the sky and spoke to me. An angel dressed in blue with long flowing hair – "

"Well, I have never heard of any celestial beings visiting Norfolk before," the Queen sighed. "Perhaps you were a little light-headed from all the exercise?"

Arkady bowed politely.

"That was certainly the case," he said.

The King smiled.

"There is always a logical explanation," he said. "even for the most remarkable occurrences, but then Count Dimitrov, we must take care to keep you entertained while you stay with us. We cannot run the risk of losing you to another ethereal visitation, when there are so many pretty girls among our neighbouring families. We must give a ball for you, Count."

Arkady was pretty sure that he heard the Queen give a little sigh of pleasure and certainly her face seemed to glow in the candlelight.

"A very good idea," she said. "I always welcome any opportunity to bring guests to our ballroom for a little music and dancing."

The King and Queen were both quite portly now and well past middle age. But Arkady had a sudden vision of them in their younger years, enthusiastically partnering each other in waltzes and polkas.

Their kindness to him was undoubted, although he could not help thinking, that he would rather spend another five minutes in the company of the lovely blue-eyed angel with the wild dark hair he had met by the sea than a long night of dancing with the local beauties.

His reverie was interrupted by the entrance of the butler to announce that dinner was served.

"Come Count, you must have your fill of our best English roast beef," the King said, as they walked into the dining room. "It will keep the angels from bothering you!"

But Arkady found he had no appetite for rich food that night. His mind and heart were filled with a strange ecstasy, a vivid vision of blue sky and golden sand and a white horse racing towards him.

*

Chiara woke next morning with an uncomfortable feeling in her heart.

Mervyn Hunter's last words were ringing inside her head, "*it will not be long before we meet again!*"

She did not want to see him.

She could not forget how he had seized the reins from her, making Erebus fall and then blamed the little pony for throwing her.

She found this thought so troubling that she spoke of it to her Mama over breakfast.

"I cannot believe that Mr. Hunter would do such a thing. He was so worried about you," Lady Fairfax said. "As soon as you failed to return to the drawing room and the groom told us you had gone out for a ride, he insisted that he should come and find you."

"I do not think it was quite gentlemanly of him to make my horse lose his footing. He blamed Erebus for my fall just to make himself look like a hero."

Lady Fairfax frowned and put down her coffee cup.

"Are you quite sure? It was almost dark. Perhaps you did not see exactly what happened. Mr. Hunter told me that Erebus ran away with you across the fields."

"No, no, Mama!"

Chiara explained that she had just been taking a short cut, because she wanted to return to Rensham Hall as soon as she could.

"I cannot believe, my darling, that he would have taken such a risk – why, you could have been badly hurt."

Chiara shivered.

"Yes, Mama. I was lucky and Erebus *was* hurt. He is very lame."

Lady Fairfax sighed.

"Perhaps it is for the best. It might be wise if you did not go on any more of these wild rides."

Chiara was about to protest, when the butler entered with a folded note on a small silver tray. He bent down so that Lady Fairfax could take the note.

"Lord Darley is coming to take me for a drive!"

Lady Fairfax was on her feet in an instant, a warm blush of excitement lighting up her face.

Chiara caught her breath, thinking that his friend, Mervyn Hunter, might be coming too. But Lady Fairfax was reading the rest of the note.

"Oh, there is a message here for you, Chiara. Mr. Hunter has been called away to an important race meeting, but sends his compliments and most sincerely hopes that you have recovered from your mishap last night."

"There would have been no mishap, Mama, if he had not come chasing after me."

"Chiara – " Lady Fairfax began, about to reprimand her daughter, but then she paused and looked thoughtful before continuing,

"My darling, Mr. Hunter – is very fond of you, I think. It may be that he cares for you so very much that it caused him to behave somewhat foolishly, perhaps in his excitement he misread the situation. I am sure that he did not mean you any harm. Quite the opposite. Please, my darling, try to think of him a little more kindly."

She then turned and left the dining room, hurrying to meet Lord Darley.

Chiara went up to her bedroom and sat on the sofa.

She found the letter Elizabeth had sent her, where she wrote about Mervyn Hunter.

"*You say that he is very handsome. Have you been thinking about him? It could be love!*"

Perhaps her Mama was right and he did care for her. He was certainly handsome and she did find herself thinking about him – he had been in her mind since the moment she awoke this morning.

But when she thought more about him, she felt not happy and joyful, but angry and anxious. If this was love, it was not a pleasant sensation at all.

*

A few days later, Mervyn Hunter watched from the Grandstand at Epsom as the horse he had trained, which was the favourite to win the race, suddenly seemed to lose speed and fell back from first place to finish fifth.

He then lowered his binoculars and cursed under his breath.

"Oh, bad luck!" Mrs. Fulwell, who had come to the meeting with him, slid her arm through her brother's.

"Hmph! It's the jockey's fault, lazy little tyke. He seems to have no idea what to do with his whip. Come, I shall have words with him."

They made their way through the colourful crowd of excited racegoers to the unsaddling enclosure.

Reuben Jones, a small wizened man, who had won many races over his long career, shook his head as Mervyn Hunter shouted at him.

"He 'ad nothin' left to give, guv'nor. He was worn out as we came into the final furlong. He's a good 'orse, but you've trained 'im too 'ard," the little man said.

"I did not ask for your opinion, Jones, and I would thank you to keep it to yourself," Mervyn Hunter growled. "If you ride one of my horses again, I shall expect you to follow my instructions and use your whip! That's the way to get results."

The Jockey shrugged and backed away.

"If you say so, guv'nor."

The tired and sweating horse was led away, its head hanging low in defeat and weariness.

"What a shame, Mervyn." Mrs. Fulwell squeezed her brother's arm. "You are a man of such talents, you just need a little luck."

"What I do need," he replied, his thin lips curled angrily, "is a good stables and fine gallops to work the horses on. I am sick to death of trying to train winners in whatever rough corner of farmland I can get someone to loan out to me."

"Cannot Lord Darley do anything to help you?"

"Ha!" he gave a disdainful little laugh. "I had some hopes there, I may say, but, as you well know, his Lordship is a younger son. He might well be a Lord, but he's hardly got two farthings to rub together."

"Oh, what a shame. He really is such an amiable young man and so handsome. I was hoping he might be here today."

Mervyn Hunter gave a little smile.

"His Lordship has realised the folly of trying to win wagers on the racetrack and I think he has fallen in love."

"Oh, no!" Mrs. Fulwell laughed. "My girls will be upset. They both adore him, though, of course, I have told them that without a substantial fortune to offer them, he is quite out of bounds. Who is she?"

"A wealthy widow. Older than he is, but not bad-looking."

"Mervyn!" Mrs. Fulwell shook her brother's arm. "You have missed an opportunity there, letting him get to her first!"

"She has eyes only for him. From the first moment they met. But I would not have let him get away with it so easily, if the lady did not have a very pretty daughter."

"*Oh, Mervyn*!" Mrs. Fulwell gave a little squeal.

He grinned at her.

"Now, sister, you are letting your imagination run ahead of you," he said. "Though I must say, I find myself doing the same!"

He shut his eyes for a moment, picturing the wide sweep of the Park at Rensham Hall and a string of elegant racehorses galloping over it.

"Has she fallen for you?" Mrs. Fulwell asked, her blue eyes bulging with excitement.

"Oh, I rather think she hates me at present. She is young and naïve and has been very much left to have her own way. But I will bring her to her senses soon enough."

"Of course you will, dear Mervyn. There isn't a girl alive who can hold out against your charms for long. And, if Lord Darley marries her mother – "

"Exactly. It will be easier to make the daughter mine. To say nothing of the stables and the best expanse of old turf in East Anglia! I shall hold back for a bit, until Darley has his feet under the table and then I will make my move."

"You may not have won this race, but I think we should celebrate," Mrs. Fulwell crowed. "I can see a bright future ahead for you, dear brother."

And the two of them were smiling broadly as they set off in search of a bottle of champagne.

*

"My dear Tom!" Lady Fairfax said to Lord Darley, as they sat in her drawing room a few days later. "I am all of a dither!"

"But why, my pet?"

"The King is inviting all the local Society families to Sandringham. He is holding a ball. But I really don't think that I should go."

"Nonsense! Of course you should."

"But Tom, without you, I shall be completely and utterly miserable."

Lord Darley threw back his head and laughed.

"My dear old Papa was a very good friend of the King. He used to stay at our house in Pembrokeshire when I was a child. I am sure he would not mind if I turn up with Lord and Lady Duckett. After all, I am their guest and I have been staying there for so long I am practically one of their family."

"That would be divine!" Lady Fairfax sighed. "We shall be able to dance together."

Lord Darley took her hand.

"I cannot wait. You were a dancer in Italy before you married Lord Fairfax, weren't you? I hope I shall be able to keep up with you."

"Of course you will!"

They gazed into each other's eyes for a moment.

"And Chiara must come as well, of course," Lord Darley suddenly said.

"Yes! She has the loveliest dress she brought back from Ely. It will be an opportunity for her to shine."

Lady Fairfax's eyes lit up.

"What a shame Mervyn is so busy with his horses at the moment," Lord Darley added. "He should so much like to partner her."

"Yes. We have seen so little of him recently. But – Tom, I think perhaps it is just as well. For he adores her and I think she does not quite appreciate him."

"You are so wise, my pet. Let's hope that absence makes her heart grow fonder, as they say it does."

"Oh, Tom! Promise me that you are not going to go away just yet! If I grow any fonder of you, I think I shall not be able to bear it!" Lady Fairfax cried and put her head on his shoulder.

Lord Darley sat back on the sofa and smiled, as if he had no intention of leaving Rensham Hall ever again.

CHAPTER SIX

Every single day Chiara visited Erebus in the small paddock where he was recovering from his fall, bringing him pocketfuls of sugar lumps, peppermints and carrots to cheer him up.

One afternoon, about a week after the accident, she noticed that he no longer flinched when he stepped on his sprained leg.

"You are getting better now. Is it all the treats I have been giving you?" she asked, patting him. Then she noticed that someone had tied a poultice of dark leaves around the pony's fetlock.

"That's my doing, my Lady. I put it on his leg," Jonah said, when she asked him if he knew anything about the poultice.

"But whatever is it?"

"Boneset, my Lady. My grandmother grows it in her garden."

"Boneset?"

Chiara had never heard of it.

Jonah nodded.

"Grandma says it can help any broken bone or bad sprain to heal. There isn't much growin' this early in the year, but I found a few plants in the kitchen garden."

He went into the harness room and came out with a handful of pointed leaves.

"Careful, Lady Chiara," he said, as she reached out to take them. "Best not to touch. See, those little hairs that grow on the leaf might irritate your hand. But it's a real powerful healer. 'Russian comfrey' the gardener calls it, but I always likes to call it 'boneset'."

"How very extraordinary, it certainly seems to have helped poor Erebus. His lameness is almost gone."

Jonah nodded.

"You'll be ridin' him again before too long, your Ladyship."

Chiara sighed.

"I hope so. Mama is worried that he will take off with me again. I think Mr. Hunter has turned her against him."

Jonah's face darkened and Chiara could tell that the mention of that gentleman's name upset him.

"You don't like him, do you Jonah? But at least he has not visited us again since the accident. Mama says he is away at the races."

The groom nodded, but said nothing and Chiara did not pursue the subject.

Mervyn Hunter was much on her mind today, as he would be attending the ball at Sandringham tonight. Lord and Lady Duckett had arranged an invitation for him along with Lord Darley.

There was no doubt that he would ask her to dance with him and how could she then refuse without seeming foolish and very impolite?

What if he should try to kiss her again?

A little shudder passed over her and she felt once more the hot pressure of his lips against hers. Even the memory of that moment was enough to make her blush.

"Your Ladyship!" A maid came running over to the paddock gate, her white apron flapping around her. "Lady Fairfax is askin' for you."

It was time to go in.

Chiara's mother would need help with her toilette and would insist on seeing and approving her daughter's gown and accessories.

Chiara sighed and sent up a fervent little prayer that Mervyn Hunter might have met another girl at the races and forgotten all about her.

*

Arkady shook a few drops from the silver bottle of hair dressing his mother, the Dowager Countess, had given him before he left Russia.

He held the drops in his palm for a moment and let the exotic scent of spices and green limes fill his nose.

He was filled with a sudden longing for his home.

The ice would be melting now on the river and the snow disappearing from the roof of his Palace in a gurgling torrent of melting water.

He should be there now. If it was not for this ball tonight that the King and Queen had so kindly decided to honour him with, he would have left already and would be on board ship looking out over a wild tossing seascape.

He had been down to the beach again many times, on the brand new bicycle His Majesty had so thoughtfully provided for his use and gazed out over the white-topped waves in the direction of Russia, so many miles beyond.

But what had become of the ethereal tousle-haired angel on the little white horse?

It was not that he needed the ragged coat back – the gardener's boy had been given a fine new tweed to replace it, but Arkady had felt sure that the beautiful angel would return it.

And he wanted to speak to her again, hear her soft voice and marvel once more at how skilfully she could ride her spirited horse.

But there it was.

Perhaps, after all, she was just a weird vision, an enchanted but tantalising figment of his imagination.

There would be a crowd of pretty girls tonight to distract him and he could flirt with them to his heart's content, knowing that in a few days he would be gone and would never have to see any of them again.

He rubbed his palms together and then smoothed the scented lotion through his dark hair.

He was ready, down to the last detail, to make his appearance in the ballroom.

*

"So how do I look?" Lady Fairfax anxiously patted her elegant coiffure with her gloved hand, as they stood in the elegant cloakroom at Sandringham. "I am afraid that we have come much too early, there are hardly any other guests – "

"You are perfect," Chiara reassured her, admiring her Mama's neat figure, swathed in a shimmering gown of turquoise silk.

"No, Darling – *you* are perfect!" Lady Fairfax said, with a little sigh. "You are just at that age, so young and yet so grown up and that white gown is utterly divine. Do you have your ball card?"

Chiara nodded.

The card, with the list of all the dances and blank spaces beside them for those who wished to partner her to write their names in, was safely tucked at her waist.

She smoothed down the soft skirt of the dress that Elizabeth had so kindly given her. She could feel already how it would swirl around her when she danced.

A stately footman approached them as they left the cloakroom. He bowed politely and conducted them to the ballroom.

Chiara caught her breath in surprise as they walked into the brightly-lit almost empty space.

The walls were decorated with intricate flowerlike patterns made up of dazzling displays of muskets, spears and swords. It was a most unusual effect.

Queen Alexandra was at the door, welcoming her guests with Regal charm and the soft light from the many candelabra glinted on her jewelled tiara.

"Lady Fairfax, how well you are looking. And how delightful that you should be one of the first to arrive," she said in her deep mellow voice. "But who is this? It cannot be your little daughter!"

Lady Fairfax blushed.

"It is, ma'am. I can scarcely believe it myself."

Chiara's Mama was interrupted by the arrival of the King, his plump hand resting upon the shoulder of a tall dashing man with dark hair.

"Lady Fairfax," the King began. "May I introduce our Guest of Honour this evening? He is staying with us to sample the many delights of life in the English countryside. Count Arkady Dimitrov."

The man bowed, his loose dark hair falling forward over his forehead.

Then, when he had straightened up, his eyes looked piercingly into Chiara's.

"*Enchanté*," he said and the sound of his voice sent shock waves through her whole body.

She now gazed at his handsome face, at his sharp cheekbones and long curving eyebrows.

Everything about this man was immaculate from the thin gold braid that trimmed his evening coat to the faint scent of lime and spice that seemed to waft from his black hair.

And his manners and deportment were aristocratic in the extreme.

It could not be him – and yet she was quite sure that this was the ruffian who had accosted her on the beach.

Chiara's mother was squeezing her arm to remind her of her manners.

She pulled herself together and made a low curtsey, murmuring the appropriate words of greeting.

There was then a flurry of activity as more guests arrived and somehow Chiara found herself walking away from the door, her hand upon the Count's arm.

He was silent, looking sideways at her with his dark eyes, as he led her to a gilt sofa at the side of the ballroom.

Above their heads, soft music was playing from the Musician's Gallery and now their Majesties were stepping into the middle of the ballroom, circling the floor in a slow waltz to a little ripple of applause.

"*It is you*," the Count murmured and Chiara felt as if she had been waiting all her life to hear him speak those words in his deep extraordinary voice. "You are not a real angel, after all, just a young girl who goes to balls!"

He raised one of his long eyebrows, waiting for her to answer him, but she could only nod her head.

She felt shy and stupid and clumsy.

He shifted position, moving so that he was face to face with her and now she found herself with one hand on his shoulder and the other clasped in his hand.

"Well – since I am the Guest of Honour," Arkady said, "I had better take the floor for the first dance and I think you must join me."

"Oh!" Chiara gave a little cry of surprise as he spun her around, drawing her into the sensual rhythm of the waltz.

Her feet knew the steps of the waltz to perfection.

From earliest childhood her Mama had taught her and she was grateful that the dancing master at school had drilled her, as all she could focus on was the man whose hand rested so lightly on the middle of her back.

She had never danced a waltz like this before, so swift, so light and with so many turns and twists.

Around and around the Count led her, flying faster and faster across the ballroom floor, spinning her until her skirts swirled out like flower petals and her head was full of a jumble of candlelight and the glow of his dark eyes.

Her heart was racing and her whole body sang with joy. To dance like this was the most wonderful thing she had ever experienced.

It was almost exactly the same feeling as the wild exhilaration of galloping along the beach – but no, it was even better than that, for there was music. And there was – *him*.

As she thought it, the tempo of the waltz began to slow. The first dance was coming to an end.

The Count released her and bowed low at the exact spot by the gilt sofa, where they had begun to dance.

More guests were coming into the ballroom and Chiara was becoming uncomfortably aware, now that she was standing still, that most of them were looking at her.

"You are upset. What is wrong?" the Count asked, and then he gave a little shrug. "Ah! I suppose I should have reserved you by writing my name in your little card."

"No, not at all – it doesn't matter!" Chiara said quickly.

"That is the way it is done," the Count was saying now, his eyes looking into hers. "I apologise."

"No – it was wonderful!"

Chiara wanted more than anything to dance with him again. She wanted to give him her ball card and have him write his name, Count Arkady Dimitrov, beside every waltz, polka and redowa printed there.

His eyes brightened and he smiled at her.

"Perhaps you *have* flown in, after all, from the sky! I can see now that you are the same angel I saw swooping along the sands – "

"Darling!" Chiara's mother was now approaching, closely followed by Lord Darley, who had just entered the ballroom. "Our friends have arrived – you must come and say 'hello'."

Lady Fairfax's cheeks were positively glowing with excitement. All her earlier nervousness had vanished, now that Lord Darley was at her side.

Chiara was desperately torn.

She could not bear to leave the Count, as it felt to her as if he was the only person in the ballroom.

Lady Fairfax noticed her daughter's hesitation.

"Do forgive me, Count Dimitrov," she said, with a quick curtsey. "So gracious of you to honour Chiara with the first dance."

He inclined his head politely, but before he could speak, their Majesties were at hand, inviting him to meet Lord and Lady Duckett and their visitor, Lord Darley.

Suddenly Chiara's left hand was caught in a strong grasp that pulled her away from the party and towards the gilt sofa.

Mervyn Hunter had arrived and he then pressed her gloved fingers to his lips.

"Too long!" he murmured.

She felt suddenly faint and the rosettes of weapons that were pinned to the walls of the ballroom seemed to spin and whirl.

"I should be very angry with you for giving the first waltz to that Russian Count," he said in a low voice, his breath tickling her ear. "But it was such a rare pleasure to watch you dance. You are utterly lovely this evening."

"You are too kind," Chiara managed to say, though her lips felt stiff and numb.

"Now – to business! Is that your ball card I see peeping out from your pretty blue sash?"

Chiara flinched as Mervyn Hunter took the card, his fingers brushing her waist. He seemed to have no manners at all, as now he was examining it and surely this was not correct behaviour for a gentleman.

"I have struck lucky! You are still free for every dance," he crowed. "Lady Chiara, let me take them all!"

"No! You will not!"

The words sprang from out of Chiara's mouth with a vehemence she could not control. She *must* remember where she was.

She took a deep breath and began again,

"Mr. Hunter, if you would be so kind as to return my card to me, I shall be happy to fill in your name as my partner. But – I cannot give every dance to you. That would be very rude to all the other gentlemen who wish to dance with me."

To her surprise, he burst out laughing.

"I stand corrected, Lady Chiara!" he chuckled. "I am so glad that I have you to remind me how to behave or I might make a fool of myself in this august company."

He winked at her and his eyes darted to where the King and Queen were speaking to Lord and Lady Duckett.

Chiara looked at them too and she could see that the Count was there, watching her. She could not read the expression in his eyes, but she wished that Mervyn Hunter was not standing so close to her, holding her ball card in one hand and her fingers in the other.

Then the Queen beckoned to a group of young girls to join them and, as they thronged around the Count, curtseying and clutching their ball cards, he turned away from Chiara.

Mervyn Hunter was now busy insisting that at least every *other* dance should be his.

"I shall not give you a moment's peace until it is written in your card," he muttered.

Other gentlemen then came flocking over to Chiara, praising her skill as a dancer and begging to partner her.

She could not refuse them and before long her card was completely full and she knew that there was no chance that she would be able to fly across the ballroom with the Count again.

But at least she would now have some respite from Mervyn Hunter's attentions. He was not a good dancer in spite of his long legs, as his movements were too stilted and more than once she felt his boot crunch against her foot.

And his hands were too heavy and leaden as they steered her around the floor.

Waltzing with the Count, they had spun around as if they were one being, but with Mervyn Hunter she felt as if she was a parcel being tossed about by a delivery boy.

More than once she had caught the Count watching her, especially when there was a break in the music and ice cream and other refreshments were brought in.

Mervyn Hunter left her side for a moment to fetch a plate of delicacies for her. And, for a moment, the Count, who was talking to Lord Duckett, looked as if he might come and speak to her again.

But Mervyn Hunter was swiftly back at her side.

"Grapes! At this time of year?" he said. "What a world of elegance and luxury I have stepped into. I could become accustomed to such extravagance, I think – with very little difficulty."

He winked at Chiara and she smelt whisky on his breath. He must have had a quick drink while he was away from her.

The Count turned back to Lord Duckett, his arching brows pulled together in a frown.

The night seemed to go on forever, as Chiara was propelled around the ballroom floor by Mervyn Hunter and innumerable other gentlemen, whose names she could not remember.

Her feet were sore from being trodden on and her head ached.

Midnight passed and still they danced on.

Then the King called for breakfast to be brought in.

Mervyn Hunter, who by now reeked most strongly of whisky, went in search of sausages and eggs and then Chiara's mother came up, her pretty cheeks flushed red.

"Well, my darling. Your very first ball! You have outshone all the other girls. I hope that you have enjoyed yourself."

Lady Fairfax's eyes were brighter than Chiara had ever seen them.

"Thank you, Mama. I have had a very nice time," she said. She could not help looking over Lady Fairfax's shoulder to try and catch sight of the Count, but he was nowhere to be seen.

"Oh, my darling, I know that I should perhaps wait to tell you this, but I simply don't think I can!"

Lady Fairfax was whispering, her face very close to Chiara's.

"Lord Darley, my dear sweet Tom – has asked me to be his wife!"

"Mama!" Chiara choked.

"Yes! I am so happy, darling. I thought, when I lost your Papa that I should never feel joy again, but oh, now I think I must be the happiest woman in the world!"

"But – "

Chiara shook her head in disbelief.

"I know it must seem very sudden to you, darling. But we love each other so much."

"That's wonderful, Mama. Congratulations!" she managed to say.

At the side of the ballroom beneath a vast display of muskets, she could see Lord Darley, sitting on one of the small gilt sofas.

He really was a very handsome man with his dark curly hair and fresh complexion. As so often, there was a wide smile on his face.

Mama could not wish for a more good-humoured husband, Chiara reflected.

But her heart sank as she could see Mervyn Hunter sitting beside him, his long legs stretched out and his thin mouth stretched in a drunken lop-sided smile of his own.

Something about that smile then struck fear into her heart and the ballroom seemed unbearably hot and stuffy, especially now that breakfast had been brought in and the smell of fried sausages filled the air.

"I am very happy for you, Mama," Chiara said and squeezed Lady Fairfax's hand. "I am sure that Lord Darley will be a very good husband. It really is very hot in here, would you like to step outside for a little air?"

She had to get out of the ballroom at all costs.

"Oh no, my darling, I must go back to Tom. Come and have some breakfast with us."

Lady Fairfax was already heading back towards the sofa and it was easy for Chiara to slip away and go out into the cold freshness of the garden.

She was now astonished to see the sky beginning to lighten and turn grey in the East.

It was morning and she had been up all through the night dancing.

'I should be happy,' she said to herself. 'I have had my first ball and for every dance there was someone who wanted to be my partner and I have received nothing but compliments on my dress and my appearance, yet my heart feels so tired and heavy.'

She walked along the side of the house, looking for a quiet spot and breathed in the fresh cold air, trying to forget the sight of Mervyn Hunter lolling on the sofa next to the man who was going to be her stepfather.

The morning sky now began to change from grey to pink and then suddenly Chiara's whole body thrilled with excitement as she heard a strangely familiar noise coming from above the steep roofs of Sandringham House.

Swans flying!

The same wild swish of wings she had heard when she walked out over the Fens at Ely. This was much louder and there must be many more birds passing overhead.

She looked up and saw a large flock of white swans speeding past her, their long necks outstretched and their feathers turning pink by the dawn light. They were flying towards the sea.

There was a rustle of movement beside her and a footstep crunched on the gravel. Her heart skipped a beat.

A dark shape was approaching.

Mervyn Hunter had followed her!

"They are flying home," a deep voice spoke from close by her shoulder.

It was the Count.

Now she caught the intoxicating aura of lime and spices that had enveloped her as they danced and warmth flooded over her skin.

"What – do you mean?" she asked.

"They know spring is coming and the ice is melting on the Steppes." His low voice was resonating through her whole body. "They are now returning to their home and to mine. Mother Russia."

"But, I thought they lived here."

Chiara recalled the family of swans she had seen at Ely.

"Some do. But these great flocks are wild swans from the far North," he told her. "When warmth comes back to the earth, they return there. As I must soon."

"Oh!" Chiara felt a sharp pain in her heart. "Do – you have to go?"

He shifted beside her and she heard him take a long breath and waited for him to speak.

"Lady Chiara!" Lord Darley's voice now rang out through the twilight of the dawn. "Are you hiding out here somewhere? Your carriage awaits!"

She jumped, startled by this sudden intrusion into the peace of the garden.

"It is you who must go," the Count sighed. "Your people are waiting."

"But I – "

She wanted to say that Lord Darley was nothing to do with her, that he was not one of her 'people'. But then she remembered that he would soon be her stepfather.

"Go!" the Count urged, his voice rising. "Or they will all be upon us. I wish to be alone."

"Yes, I'm sorry. But – "

Chiara struggled to find the words to tell him how much she had loved dancing with him.

Now footsteps were approaching and the Count's dark figure moved away, melting into the shrubbery.

If only she, like the swans, could climb up into the air and fly East over the sea.

If *only* she could escape.

"There you are!" Lord Darley came panting up. "I told Mervyn to come and find you, but, alas, the old devil has fallen asleep. He really is a disgrace. He promised he would keep away from the whisky, tonight of all nights. Come along, Lady Chiara, your glorious Mama is already in the carriage."

The Count had completely disappeared, leaving just a trace of his clean spicy scent in the damp morning air.

Chiara, her head heavy and her heart twisting with pain, followed Lord Darley to the front of the house, where the carriage stood, ready to take her back to Rensham Hall.

CHAPTER SEVEN

"Mama, what will happen after your wedding? Will you go to live with Lord Darley?"

Chiara hoped that the anxiety she felt did not show in her voice, as she took tea with her mother in the drawing room on the afternoon after the ball.

She simply could not imagine what it would be like to have Lord Darley sitting at table in her Papa's place every day for the rest of her life.

But then what would she do, if Mama left Rensham Hall? Surely she could not stay behind all on her own?

Lady Fairfax was shaking her head.

"Oh no, darling. Poor Tom – he does not get on at all with his elder brother, Henry, who owns the estate. We could not possibly go there. We shall stay here, of course!"

Chiara felt glad for a moment and then her body turned hot and cold as she remembered Mervyn Hunter – for surely he would become a regular visitor at Rensham Hall once Lord Darley was installed here permanently.

Her feet still smarted from where he had trodden on them last night and her stomach turned over at the memory of his whisky-scented breath, so hot on her face.

Chiara looked down at her teacup, trying to hide the tears of despair that filled her eyes.

"Oh, my darling!" Lady Fairfax got up and came to sit beside her. "You must not feel sad. Tom is the kindest of men and it is my very dearest wish that we shall all live together like one big happy family."

She took Chiara's hand and squeezed it warmly.

"Forever, my darling!" she continued. "All together at Rensham Hall!"

Lady Fairfax was smiling at her, but there was an odd look in her shining eyes, which Chiara had not seen before, as if she was hiding something.

But perhaps it was just that she was thinking about her wedding and her life with Lord Darley and she felt that she should not talk too much about this with her daughter.

An odd wild feeling rose up inside Chiara.

She could see the swans in her mind's eye, early that morning, flying out to the sea and she suddenly wanted to run out of the drawing room and keep running until she could go no further.

And then when she stopped running, she wanted the Count to be there, waiting for her and to hold her lightly and tenderly as he had done when they danced.

"Whatever is the matter, darling? You have such a strange look on your face." Lady Fairfax let go of Chiara's hand.

"It's really nothing, Mama," and Chiara tried hard to make herself smile.

"My darling, you haven't fallen for someone, have you? For one of the charming young gentlemen you were dancing with? Please tell me you haven't!"

Lady Fairfax threw her arms around her daughter.

"I cannot let you go, not just yet."

It was all so unreal, for as much as she loved her Mama and Rensham Hall, as she heard her mother's words, something deep inside Chiara wanted to escape more than anything.

"Darling, you must be very tired after last night. I am sure that's why you are looking so pale. You shall take things easy for the rest of today. We are going to be very busy tomorrow."

The odd bright look came back into her eyes and once again Chiara felt a deep sense of unease.

"Of course, Mama," she replied, trying to keep a happy expression on her face. "I shall go and lie down."

But even though her bed was soft and comfortable and the thick curtains were drawn to keep out the bright light of the spring afternoon, Chiara could not sleep.

As soon as she closed her eyes, everything swam before them and she saw again the swirling candelabra and the Count's eyes looking deeply into hers as they spun and whirled across the ballroom.

*

The next morning at breakfast, Chiara's feelings of dread and discomfort were banished by the appearance of a letter for her from Ely.

"Mama!" she cried, as she ran her eyes down the lines of Elizabeth's neat handwriting. "I am going to be a bridesmaid. Arthur has arranged leave from the Army and the wedding has been fixed. Elizabeth will be so happy."

"Well, well. And when is this to be? I am not sure I can spare you, darling."

A cloud passed over Lady Fairfax's face and she looked suddenly worried.

"It's very soon, Mama. Oh, and Elizabeth will be going to India. That is why they are getting married so quickly. Arthur has been posted out there."

"Well – I suppose you will not be away for too long and you must not forget in all the excitement that you have a much more important wedding to consider."

"Of course not, Mama. I shall be a bridesmaid twice!"

Lady Fairfax then raised her eyebrows as if she was about to say something, but, although Chiara was waiting to hear what it was, her Mama remained silent.

Chiara finished her breakfast and helped herself to a handful of sugar lumps.

She was glad to leave the table and go outside into the fresh sunny morning.

Erebus's white coat shone brightly and he showed no signs of lameness as he trotted up to the paddock gate to greet her.

She stroked his nose and whispered to him, telling him how happy she was that he was better.

But the peaceful moment was then interrupted by a clatter of hooves on the drive. Two riders were rapidly approaching Rensham Hall and Chiara's heart sank as she recognised the tall silhouette of Mervyn Hunter.

*

"I cannot believe we will not see you again!" Mrs. Fulwell's faded English-rose cheeks were crumpled with dismay. "Why, I have called to invite you to join us for a visit to the Opera."

"Alas, the next time I sit down in a theatre it will be the Maryinsky!" Arkady said and his heart felt suddenly winged and light at the thought of the long journey he was about to begin.

And he mused about the glorious Maryinsky, the most famous theatre in Russia, where the very best singers and dancers in the world performed before the Czar and Czarina and all the assembled Nobility.

"You are so impulsive, Count," Mrs. Fulwell was saying. "Why, you have only just returned from your visit to Sandringham. Marigold and Eglantine will be absolutely desolate. They have been so looking forward to seeing you again."

'So who can she be talking about?' Arkady thought and then he remembered the two awkward fair-haired girls who had come to visit a few weeks previously and who had spluttered so impolitely over their glasses of Russian tea.

He had completely forgotten about them. He looked at Mrs. Fulwell, disappointment so clearly written on her face and realised that she had been hoping he might fall in love with one of her girls.

Would he ever escape the ceaseless attentions from mothers desperate to foist their unmarried daughters upon him?

And Mrs. Fulwell was not even a member of the aristocracy. She was setting her ambitions very high.

He felt a twitch of amusement.

"Well, *madame*, you must look me up when you are in St. Petersburg. My mother, the Dowager Countess, will be very delighted to make your acquaintance."

He could not believe that this little Englishwoman would ever manage the long journey to Russia. The very thought of her and her silly daughters entering the great salon at his Palace!

The expression on his mother's aristocratic face, if they should suddenly arrive and announce themselves as his guests! That would soon put them to flight!

The laughter that bubbled up inside him subsided and a sweet painful vision sprang up in its place.

The beautiful dark-haired angel, so slim and so wild and so exquisite in her soft white dress, would not be out of place in the salon. She would easily meet the noble gaze of the Countess with perfect grace.

"Why, Count! That is most generous of you." Mrs. Fulwell's face was pink with pleasure. "I shall certainly do so, if we ever come to Russia."

The Count bowed and made his profuse apologies. The butler would bring coffee for her, but he could not stay to enjoy her company. He must prepare for the journey.

He left the drawing room, his mind still full of the enchanting angel he had danced with. If only it had been she who had come to take tea with him.

He pictured her, sitting gracefully on the sofa in this cramped London drawing room, her tea glass held in her slender hand and her magical blue eyes fixed on his, full of the wildness and beauty of the open sea and sky.

If she was here this afternoon, he would not be in such a hurry to leave. But then the voice of reason spoke up, banishing his daydream,

'Arkady, you are a complete idiot. She is nothing but a frivolous English Society girl – a little prettier than the rest, maybe, and a better horsewoman!

'She belongs with that crowd of drunken fools who fell about on the dance floor. You are deceiving yourself, if you think she is anything more.'

His heart shrank inside him, but he could not ignore the scenes he had witnessed in the ballroom. The sooner he was back in St. Petersburg, the better.

*

"Sweetheart! Why are you being so distant?"

Mervyn Hunter's cold eyes were fixed on Chiara's face, as he stood with his booted legs wide apart on the carpet in front of the drawing room fire.

She flinched at the sound of the word 'sweetheart'.

But he was behaving with unexpected politeness and formality. There was no trace of the awful lop-sided,

95

drunken grin she had seen on his face last night and he was freshly shaved and wearing a smart suit.

They were alone together in the drawing room.

Lady Fairfax and Lord Darley were in the garden, discussing some new arrangements of plants. Chiara could see them, wandering amongst the flowerbeds and holding hands, from where she stood by the window.

"How can I speak properly to you when you are on the other side of the room?" Mervyn Hunter was saying.

"I hear you perfectly," Chiara replied coldly.

He frowned at her and slapped his boot with the riding crop he carried. She did not like the sudden angry expression in his eyes and turned to look outside.

"What I have to say to you, Chiara, is important. I am not prepared to say it to your back, charming as it is."

An unpleasant tone was creeping into his voice.

She heard his boots squeak as he came towards her and could not help a shiver as she felt his breath on the back of her neck.

And then his hands were on her elbows, twisting her around to face him.

"You must know how I feel about you," he said in a low voice.

Chiara closed her eyes, blocking out his face and his fierce cold stare.

"It was agony to be away from you for so long," he continued. "And then to see you at the ball, so exquisite in your white gown and I realised – "

"Please, let me go!" she cried, twisting away from him, but he renewed his firm grip on her arms, pressing her back against the window frame.

"I just cannot live without you!" Mervyn Hunter breathed.

He seized her hand and crushed it against his lips.

Then, still holding her so that she could not move, he dropped to his knees.

"I adore you," he sighed. "I must have you for my wife."

"No, *no*!"

A black tide of horror rose up inside her head as he pulled her down towards him.

"Oh – look at you! Sweet creature – half swooning with bliss!" he continued, pressing his mouth against her forehead.

"I cannot – I don't – " she struggled against the tide of darkness that pulled her down.

"You can, you shall!" he said and now his lips were pushing against hers, demanding and impulsive. "You are mine!"

Her ears were ringing and she felt as if her soul was leaving her body, drifting up towards the ceiling, as the darkness overcame her mind and she fell to the carpet in a dead faint.

"Poor child!" Chiara heard his voice, as if he was a long way off at the end of a dark tunnel and her stomach turned over with revulsion. "She is completely overcome with excitement."

A sharp whiff of smelling salts burned her nose and then she felt a soft cushion being placed under her head and her mother's soft hand holding hers.

"Oh, darling, are you feeling better?" Lady Fairfax asked. "The colour seems to be coming back into your cheeks."

Chiara opened her eyes.

The three of them, her Mama, Mervyn Hunter and Lord Darley were all standing over her.

"I-I am fine," she managed to say, although she felt very weak and sick.

"I believe that congratulations may be in order!" Lord Darley piped up.

Chiara shook her head, trying to clear her mind.

"What?"

"Darling! Has is slipped your mind that Mr. Hunter has just proposed to you!" her Mama laughed with delight. "We are so thrilled for you!"

"No – I – " Chiara stammered.

"You cannot have forgotten, darling. It was just a few moments ago."

Chiara forced herself to sit up.

"Mama – I remember – "

Then she had to close her eyes, struggling to keep herself from fainting again, as she now recalled the heat of Mervyn Hunter's lips against hers.

"But – I – don't – "

"We must not rush things," Mervyn Hunter's voice rang in her ears. "It's easy to forget that the charming creature we saw at the ball is still very young and how innocent! My poor sweetheart."

Chiara then felt his rough hand replace her Mama's, crushing her fingers tightly.

"You must rest," he suggested. "I shall cease from plaguing you with all my devoted attentions until you are feeling stronger, my love."

He dropped her hand and Chiara could hear him speaking to Lord Darley, their voices dwindling to a faint murmur as they left the drawing room.

"Whatever is wrong, Chiara?" Lady Fairfax asked, bending over her. "Are you ill? I have never seen you like this before. I should have thought you would be radiant with happiness. Your very first proposal! And from such a delightful gentleman."

"Mama – I am quite well – "

Chiara's voice felt thick in her throat, but she had to speak the truth.

"But – I don't like Mr. Hunter. I cannot – "

"*Not like him?*" Lady Fairfax's face fell. "But, my darling, he is Tom's best friend!"

"He is not quite – I don't like – "

How could she explain to her Mama the terrible distress that she felt when Mervyn Hunter touched her and thrust his lips against hers?

"Oh, my dearest Chiara!" Lady Fairfax was smiling again. "I think I can understand you. Mr. Hunter is a very *passionate* gentleman – he is so in love with you and he cannot help but show you his feelings very strongly. And, darling, perhaps that is a little too shocking for you. As he says, you are very young."

"Mama – *I don't like him!*"

Chiara felt her breath grow tight with panic.

"Oh, my darling!" Lady Fairfax was laughing now. "You will soon get used to him, believe me. We must just give you a little time."

Somehow it was more difficult to argue against her mother's amusement than if she had been angry and Chiara felt so weak and confused that she decided to say no more.

"Don't fret, my darling, all will be well!"

She then smoothed Chiara's hair back away her forehead.

"Just think – you and I have both had a proposal of marriage in the last few days – isn't that a wonderful thing?

You must not be afraid if you are not quite ready – there is no rush."

And with that Chiara had to be content.

*

"This is a very unexpected pleasure. What brings you to London, brother?"

Mrs. Fulwell greeted Mervyn Hunter with a kiss on his cheek, hiding her strong irritation that he should turn up unannounced like this.

Fond as she was of him, she could not help but think how out of place he looked in the tiny sitting room of her rented flat cluttered as it was with embroidery frames and ladies' magazines.

And she was sure that she could detect a whiff of horse coming from his riding boots.

"I've been thrown out!" he spluttered.

"What? But Mervyn – I thought the girl was yours for the taking. Has she turned you down?"

"She's playing hard to get. Little fool."

"Oh, no! Is all lost?"

"Mama says give her time and she'll come round."

He sighed and slumped down on the sofa.

"It's a poor outlook for me, if Tom gets hitched to Lady Fairfax and the daughter gives me the cold shoulder."

"She could not wish for a better man than you, my dear brother."

"Absolutely and she's not had much chance to look at the competition. Only been to one ball that I know of."

"We must keep it that way, Mervyn. We don't want any other gentlemen sneaking past the post first."

A little smile crept onto Mrs. Fulwell's face. An interesting idea had occurred to her.

"I would like to meet this Lady Fairfax. Perhaps I should take the girls to Norfolk for a visit."

Mervyn Hunter's eyebrows shot up.

"I thought you had a big fish to fry in London."

"No, alas. The Russian Count has returned home. I would follow, but I don't have the funds to take the three of us."

"Then yes – why not go to Norfolk. Lady Fairfax will be delighted, I am sure. Your girls will be company for the precious Lady Chiara and you can keep an eye on the little minx for me."

"I should love to do that for you, brother. She is still very young, as you say. Perhaps you have been a little too – how shall I put it – manly for her taste, my dear. But I am sure she'll come round. I will do my best to plead your cause. And you may stay here, while we are away."

Mervyn Hunter lay back on the sofa and stretched out his boots to the fire that flickered in the tiny grate.

"Your grasp of tactics is as good as ever, sister," he said. "You would have made a first-rate General."

Mrs. Fulwell sniffed.

"I should rather be a lady and live a life of ease and comfort," she said. "I am very tired of this life – struggling to make ends meet. It's now time things came good for us, brother."

Mervyn Hunter nodded his hearty agreement as his sister went to make tea for him.

*

"It really is exceedingly inconsiderate of Elizabeth to decide to get married now," Lady Fairfax puffed. "There is so much to do for my own wedding and we have guests arriving tomorrow."

Chiara was packing her trunk to return to Ely for a few days.

"It's the only time that Arthur is free, Mama. You know that and if Elizabeth is to go to India with him, I may not see her again for many years. I *must* go."

"Well, I can only hope that your friend will be able to persuade you of the advantages of accepting the sincere attentions of a gentleman who cares for you as deeply as Mr. Hunter does."

A chill ran over Chiara's skin, as it always did when she heard that name.

"Speak with Elizabeth, darling. She is more mature and experienced than you are. Let her talk some sense into you," Lady Fairfax burbled on.

"Yes, Mama. I am sure we will not be able to stop talking – it's so long since we have seen each other."

That, at least, was true, Chiara thought. But what would Elizabeth make of Mervyn Hunter?

She closed the lid of her trunk and snapped the lock together. She was ready to go and her heart gave a little skip of joy at the thought of seeing Ely again.

*

"Chiara. You are blushing!" Elizabeth cried. "You turn pink every time we talk about Mr. Hunter!"

The two girls were sitting side by side on the blue silk coverlet of Elizabeth's bed.

In between them lay a pile of lace petticoats that were to be folded and packed for Elizabeth's honeymoon.

"You *must* feel something for him, don't you?" she continued.

"Well, I suppose so – but it's not a pleasant feeling, Elizabeth."

Chiara could not bring herself to talk of the deep revulsion that she felt when Mervyn Hunter touched her, even to her best friend.

"How – do you feel, when Arthur – kisses you?" she asked, feeling suddenly shy.

"Oh, goodness me! I just cannot begin to describe it! Marvellous! Just all warm and loved and – "

Elizabeth wrapped her arms around herself at the thought, her eyes shining with joy.

"Do you feel – like you could fly away? When he puts his arms around you?"

Chiara remembered the ballroom at Sandringham and the Count's light touch on the small of her back as they twirled around the dance floor.

"Yes, sometimes and sometimes I just feel so safe and happy. I feel like I have 'come home', if you know what I mean."

Elizabeth frowned as she tried to put into words her deepest and most private feelings.

Chiara gave a little shudder.

"When Mervyn Hunter touches me, I feel just like I have to run away," she admitted. "I actually fainted once – when he proposed to me."

"I well remember being a little nervous sometimes, when Arthur was first in love with me. He was so strong and so loving and I did even feel quite faint once."

"But Elizabeth – I don't like him! When I see him – I feel cold. I have tried to tell Mama."

"You are going all pink again," Elizabeth reached out and took her hand. "Chiara, if you don't like him, you will never be able to love him."

"No! I cannot! I hate the way that he looks at me – there is nothing about him I like."

103

Chiara felt relief rush through her body, as she saw that Elizabeth understood and believed her.

"You cannot marry this man," her friend said. "It's a shame, as I was so very excited to hear that you had had a proposal. And I am sure your Mama feels the same way, but you cannot accept him."

"I never shall," Chiara answered, feeling very much stronger and happier now that she had Elizabeth's support. "But we must not talk any more about all that. *You* are getting married tomorrow and that is the most important thing."

*

Next day, the sun shone through the great stained glass windows of Ely Cathedral, shedding bright jewels of light over the stone floor.

But the brightest light of all shone from Elizabeth's glowing eyes, as she walked back down the wide aisle on the arm of her new husband, Arthur.

Chiara stared spellbound at her dear friend, hardly recognising the gracious woman in the cream silk gown, her red hair smoothed close to her head under the swept-back veil.

All through the Reception, she could only marvel at the endless happiness and joy that seemed to radiate out of the couple, infecting all those who came near them.

The Dean made a gracious sermon from the pulpit, but there were tears in his eyes as he made his speech at the Reception, wishing happiness and long life to his daughter and his new son-in-law.

Chiara tried to imagine herself in Elizabeth's place, with Mervyn Hunter at her side, but all she could feel was emptiness.

There would be no light of joy in his eyes, as there was now in Arthur's as he closely watched Elizabeth cut the wedding cake.

Mervyn Hunter would take Chiara as his wife in the same way that he had danced with her, roughly and impetuously, without care or kindness.

All too soon it was time for the couple to leave. Before she stepped into the carriage, Elizabeth raised her bouquet of white hyacinths and narcissus.

As she threw it, her eyes met Chiara's and her lips mouthed the words,

'*For you*! *Be happy*!'

And the flowers flew like a white bird through the air and landed in Chiara's outstretched hands, their sweet perfume filling the air.

CHAPTER EIGHT

"Chiara, I simply cannot believe my ears!"

Lady Fairfax sat upright on the drawing room sofa at Rensham Hall, her face a picture of disappointment.

"This is not what I was expecting to hear at all."

"I am sorry, Mama, if I have upset you. But I have to be truthful and, as I have just said, I don't want to marry Mervyn Hunter – I really cannot."

All the way back from Ely, she had been making up her mind to talk to her mother.

Now, it took all of her strength to speak firmly and calmly, when what she really wanted to do was to run out of the drawing room, escape to the stable yard and bury her face in Erebus's white mane.

The little pony would certainly not condemn her for refusing Mervyn Hunter, the man who had caused him to fall and lamed him.

"But darling, I *am* upset. I had such a lovely plan and now it will never come about." Lady Fairfax dabbed at her eyes with a lace handkerchief. "I thought we might have had a double wedding – Tom and myself and you and Mr. Hunter! We would have been the talk of Society."

Chiara did not know what to say to this thought.

It was indeed a charming idea and she would have gladly gone along with it, if only Mervyn Hunter had been someone she loved and not a man who chilled her whole being.

"Poor Tom! He was delighted by the idea," her Mama continued. "You really are causing a great deal of trouble, Chiara."

"Mama, I don't mean to be difficult, I really don't." Chiara took a deep breath to steady her voice and went on, "but I don't like Mervyn Hunter. I cannot marry him."

Lady Fairfax clasped her hands tightly in a gesture of exasperation.

"Chiara, you have just seen your best friend being married – how can you not see what a wonderful gift it is that Mr. Hunter is offering you when he asks you to be his wife."

"It's very different for Elizabeth, Mama. She *loves* Arthur and he loves her. Their love shines out of them when they are together. And – Elizabeth told me that when she is with Arthur, she feels as if she has come home. I don't feel like that at all when I am with Mervyn Hunter. I feel cold and – uncomfortable – and I cannot wait to get away from him."

"This is all unspeakably awkward," Lady Fairfax said, shaking her head. "How can you speak so unkindly of the best friend of my husband-to-be? Mr. Hunter cares for you so much and, my darling, how am I to face his sister, Mrs. Fulwell, when she comes to stay with us? How can I look her in the eye, knowing that you have said such horrid things about her brother?"

Chiara's heart sank.

"I did not know he had a sister. Why is she coming here?"

"I have invited her, as I should very much like to make her acquaintance and I do wonder, Chiara, if you are spending too much time on your own. It would be so good for you to have company of your own age. Mrs. Fulwell has two daughters."

"But we don't know them, Mama."

"We have never met, certainly. But Mr. Hunter is Tom's dearest friend and as such he is almost part of the family. Thus I am only too happy to welcome his sister to Rensham Hall."

A slow tide of despair rose up in Chiara, as she pictured her future at The Hall. Even if she did not marry Mervyn Hunter, he would always be a part of her life.

His closeness to Lord Darley, who was soon to take her Papa's place, meant he would always be a welcome visitor at her home.

And his sister and her daughters too, whatever they were like, might also become part of this new 'family' that Chiara was beginning to dread so much.

*

"How lucky you are, to have your own horse," the younger of the Misses Fulwell said a few days later, as she leant on the gate of Erebus's paddock, her pale eyes wide with envy as she watched him cropping the fresh spring grass, his coat shining white in the sunshine. "I would love to ride him – "

Chiara did not think that Erebus would take kindly to the plump girl on his back, but before she could think of a suitable reply, the elder girl interrupted.

"Marigold! Don't be ridiculous! Don't you recall what Uncle Mervyn said? The beast isn't safe! Chiara might have been killed if he had not caught the reins and stopped the brute from bolting."

"Oh, yes!" Marigold turned to stare at Chiara. "You must have been absolutely terrified, until Uncle Mervyn rescued you."

Chiara opened her mouth to tell them what had really happened and then closed it again.

Perhaps it was better for them to think that Erebus was wild and difficult. Otherwise she might have to share him with them and she really did not want to do that.

"Did he carry you home in his arms after he saved you?" Marigold asked Chiara. "All our friends in London would be so jealous, if he did. They think Uncle Mervyn is terribly handsome."

"Do be quiet," her sister scolded. "Remember what Mama told us."

Marigold gave a little giggle and pressed a finger to her lips.

"Oh, yes, Eglantine. Sensitive subject!"

Chiara's skin prickled as she realised that they must have been talking about her and Mervyn Hunter.

Their pale grey eyes reminded her of him a little, and they looked at her in the same way as he did, coldly, as if they were assessing how much she was worth.

Eglantine was eyeing her clothes.

"That dress," she enquired, "where is it from?"

Chiara glanced down at her dark woollen frock that looked very plain and simple next to Marigold's green-and-white striped poplin and Eglantine's lavender-and-red striped silk.

"It's one of the dresses I had at school," she replied.

She had become used to wearing it at home since her Papa died.

"We thought you would have all your clothes made in Paris," Eglantine said. "You are *Lady* Chiara after all!"

"And your house is absolutely *huge* too!" Marigold added, swivelling her head to count the windows along the front of Rensham Hall.

"I am sorry that my clothes have not come up to your expectations," Chiara parried.

Eglantine looked down her long nose at her.

"Well, you are quite pretty," she remarked. "But then we expected nothing less, from what Uncle Mervyn told us."

"He really does adore you," Marigold said, giggling behind her hand.

"Shhh!" Eglantine slapped her sister's arm.

Chiara's head felt suddenly tight.

However was she going to get through the coming days? The Fulwells had come to stay at Rensham Hall for a week and the two girls were getting on her nerves after only a couple of hours.

"Would you like me to show you the garden?" she asked. "There are some very fine tulips just coming out."

"If you must," Marigold said, looking bored and then added, "yes, how lovely," as Eglantine aimed another slap at her arm.

They walked along the gravel path with their gaudy dresses billowing in the breeze and Chiara followed them, longing to run to the paddock and leap on Erebus's back and gallop away together down to the sea.

*

"So, when is the wedding?"

Mrs. Fulwell sipped her tea and directed her gaze at Lady Fairfax.

It was hard to keep her eyes from darting around the drawing room. There was so much exquisite china on the mantelpiece, so many valuable gold and silver trinkets displayed on the shelves!

Her Ladyship had no right to be looking quite so unhappy. She was living in the height of luxury. Any one of these old oil paintings on the walls would have kept the

Fulwells very nicely for at least a year.

"Oh, we have not fixed a date. We were hoping for a joint wedding, you know," Lady Fairfax replied.

Mrs. Fulwell shook her head in sympathy.

"What a shame, your Ladyship! Still – young girls can be very headstrong."

"Not my Chiara, until now! She has always been the sweetest of girls – she can be a little fiery sometimes, but I think she must inherit that from me, Mrs. Fulwell – as I am Italian, you know."

"Yes, your Ladyship." Mrs. Fulwell smiled.

Both Lady Fairfax and her daughter had heads of thick dark shining hair. But Elaine Fulwell could not help but prefer her own girls' pretty straight fair hair.

As did most gentlemen, she was quite sure. A fair girl would always catch a gentleman's eye.

Now Lady Fairfax was asking her about Marigold and Eglantine. Did they have any suitors?

"Well, I am glad you brought that up, Lady Fairfax. A certain gentleman of very high birth indeed has invited us to St. Petersburg!"

That should surely impress her Ladyship!

"How marvellous! You must certainly take up the invitation. Do you think he is interested?"

Lady Fairfax was sitting up, her attention caught by Mrs. Fulwell's words.

"Without a doubt, your Ladyship. He was indeed most attentive to Eglantine."

"And does she like him?"

"Eglantine is a good girl, your Ladyship. Even if she did not like him, she would do as I advise. But the gentleman in question is very good-looking for a Russian.

111

I think he has been much in her thoughts."

"We met a Russian gentleman, a Count Dimitrov at Sandringham the other night at the King's ball. He was certainly handsome," Lady Fairfax remarked .

Mrs. Fulwell felt the blood rush to her cheeks.

"That is the very same gentleman," she exclaimed. "What a coincidence!"

What had he been doing at the ball? Had her Ladyship noticed him forming an attachment to some other girl?

But Lady Fairfax quickly put Mrs. Fulwell's mind at rest.

"He danced the first waltz with Chiara and they looked very well together," she was saying, "but he did not partner her again. And he did not speak to us all evening. He seemed very aloof. I might almost call him moody!"

Ah! So there was nothing to worry about.

Mrs. Fulwell relaxed.

"I expect he was thinking of Eglantine," she said with a little smile.

"I daresay!" Lady Fairfax reached for the silver teapot to pour her guest a second cup. "He certainly looked as if he was in another world for most of the time!"

*

Arkady was home. Now, at last, he would be able to breathe.

Here at the vast country residence that his family liked to call *The Dacha*, although it had now become more of a mansion than the simple country retreat that Peter the Great had donated to his Dimitrov ancestors.

From where he stood, in the shelter of the glass-covered veranda that ran along the front of the house, he could look out over his acres of empty grassland and vast woods with tall ancient trees.

But – *how could this be*? – the Count found his thoughts returning to the gentle rolling fields and the pretty spring flowers of the English countryside.

Spring had certainly arrived here in Russia, but the melting snow had left patches of brown grass exposed and the branches of the trees, where noisy rooks had arrived to build their nests, were still bare.

Perhaps it was this drabness in the landscape that caused his heart to feel so empty.

He was depressed, that was it. Perhaps he should have stayed in St. Petersburg after all and thrown himself into the social life there.

But he could think of only one thing that would cheer him up.

And that would be to leap upon a bicycle and pedal swiftly towards the sea –

Alas, there was no sea anywhere near to here, not for hundreds and hundreds of miles. And, should he make that long journey to the coast of the Black Sea or to the icy shores of the far North, he would be incredibly unlikely to encounter the dark-haired angel there, the girl that, try as he might, he could not put from his mind.

There was nothing for it but to be patient and wait for time to erase her memory from his mind and heart.

And to remind himself, as he did at least once a day, that by now she was probably engaged to one of the boorish English gentlemen, who had swarmed round her at the ball, like a cluster of flies in their black evening suits.

*

"What can I do to persuade you how deeply I care for you?" Mervyn Hunter was on his knees in front of

113

Chiara, gripping tightly onto the skirt of her riding habit with both hands.

They were in the stable yard in front of Erebus's box and she could not help thinking that his clean white breeches would be soiled with mud and straw when he did stand up.

"I have left you alone in consideration for your youth and innocence and I have given you ample time to consider my proposal – why will you not answer me?" he was saying, his lean face turning dark red with emotion.

Chiara kept her lips firmly closed, as to keep silent gave her a feeling of strength and she was determined this time not to let him distress her.

"Can you not see it? You *must* be my wife. It was meant to be."

His voice was growing louder and he twisted his hands in the thick cloth of her riding habit.

Across the yard Jonah was now approaching with a forkful of hay. When he saw Mervyn Hunter, he dropped the fork and came running.

"Lady Chiara! Is all well?" he called, in his lilting Norfolk accent. "Is the gentleman hurt?"

Chiara felt laughter bubble up inside her, as she realised how absurd Mervyn Hunter must look, kneeling on the dirty cobblestones.

"I really don't know, Jonah," she replied. "He has slipped and fallen at my feet!"

Mervyn Hunter's eyes now widened with anger as he heard this and before he could contradict her, Chiara stepped back and pulled her riding habit free of his grasp, so that he overbalanced and fell onto all fours.

"Be careful, sir," Jonah said. "There's been rain today and the stones be ever so slippery."

He bent and took Mervyn Hunter's arm to help him up.

"Get off!" He shook him aside angrily. "I am quite all right."

He stood up and glared at Chiara, rage flaming in his pale eyes.

"You are making fun of me!"

He was absolutely furious and yet Chiara knew that he would not dare to strike her or seize hold of her again in front of Jonah and his raging anger made the feeling of determination inside her grow stronger.

"I am simply concerned for you, Mr. Hunter," she replied.

"You are lying! How can that be so when you have so little regard for my feelings?" his voice was low now in an attempt to keep Jonah from hearing his words.

Chiara knew that the time had come, once and for all, to tell Mervyn Hunter that he must leave her alone.

Even if she had had some slight feeling for him in her heart, the last few days spent in the company of his sister and his nieces would have convinced her that she could never, never wish to be associated with his family.

"Mr. Hunter," she began, "I do indeed consider your feelings and that is why I must tell you now that I do not intend to marry you and I never will. You must not ask me again."

Jonah backed away from them, his mouth hanging open in amazement.

"How can you – speak like that to – me?" Mervyn Hunter was spluttering with rage.

"I don't like to do it," Chiara replied, "and I don't wish to do it again. So please remember what I have said."

Her limbs were shaking, but her heart swelled with

confidence as she watched him.

"But – I – "

His face was scarlet.

"Mr. Hunter, I think your relatives are with Mama in the drawing room. You may wish to change before you join them."

She glanced down at his knees and he gave a loud exclamation of annoyance, as he saw the muddy patches on his breeches.

"Good afternoon, Mr. Hunter," she said politely.

He then walked away from her towards the house, swallowing an impatient curse as he went.

"Lady Chiara!" Jonah's face was now white with shock and embarrassment. "I didn't mean to overhear – "

"It doesn't matter, Jonah. Mr. Hunter asked me to marry him, but I have turned him down and now all that is in the past. I want to forget all about it and I know that you will be discreet."

"Of course, my Lady. But I am so glad – "

Jonah bit his lip, cutting off his words.

"What do you mean? Tell me!"

"It is just that – I've seen him hangin' about here in the yard and I've overheard some of the things he has been sayin'. He has plans to bring all his racehorses here and I shouldn't have liked to work for him. He's not a good-tempered man."

Chiara laughed.

"No indeed and I wonder if it's the stables that he loves and not me after all!"

Jonah nodded.

"Well, my Lady – the Head Groom has seen him drinking' at the inn and – a-speakin' with the innkeeper's daughter."

He blushed very red.

"Let's hope then, Jonah, that she will help him to get over any hurt feelings he may have. And now – I am going to forget the whole thing and go for a ride, if Erebus is completely recovered."

"Yes, my Lady, he is, and he'll be pleased to have you take him out, he's been frettin' these last few weeks, with nothin' to do."

"I must be quick, Jonah – Mama does not like me riding after the accident and Mr. Hunter will be sure to tell her that he found me in the stable yard."

"I will saddle him up, my Lady, and you will be away in a moment," Jonah said, unbolting the stable door.

Mervyn Hunter grunted with some annoyance as he pulled his boots off in the boot room, where Mrs. Fulwell had come to find him.

"Mervyn – surely you are not going to quit?" she asked him.

"I've had it, sister. All the stable yards in England aren't worth it."

He threw his boots at the wall with another grunt.

"Lady Fairfax is *so* keen for you to marry the girl."

"That's as may be. I'm not putting myself up for any more humiliation. She just insulted me in front of the stable boy. Little minx!"

"Her Mama should know of this. Come, Mervyn, speak to her Ladyship. She's in the drawing room."

"Much good it will do," he replied. "I must look elsewhere. What about the Russian, Elaine? You have not spoken of him for a while. He'd be good for few thousand for a training establishment, don't you think?"

"I do, Mervyn. But you are forgetting – he's in St. Petersburg and myself and my girls are here in Norfolk."

He leant forward.

"Have a word with Lady Fairfax," he suggested. "You have pretty much got her in your pocket, sister. She will sponsor you, I'm sure, to have a little jaunt to Russia."

Mrs Fulwell shook her head.

"I'll try. But – if you've had no success with Lady Chiara, it may be that our days of being in favour here are numbered."

*

Chiara cantered home from the beach with the wind in her hair and a lightness in her heart that she had not felt for many days.

No ragged-coated gentleman had come down from the dunes to greet her, but she had not expected it, as she knew that the Count had left Sandringham and gone home to his native Russia.

She could not help, though, remembering his face, so striking under his loose dark hair and the sound of his voice that had resonated so powerfully through her body.

He was thousands of miles away and yet, when she thought of him, it seemed as if he might suddenly appear again and speak to her.

If only he would.

If only he was here beside her, seated on that old bicycle and the two of them could ride away through the country lanes, so that she did not have to go and sit in the stuffy drawing room and face the questions and comments of the ghastly Fulwells.

When Chiara had changed from her riding habit and reluctantly gone downstairs, she was surprised to find that only her mother was seated on the sofa. The others were nowhere to be seen.

"You look very flushed, darling," her Mama began.

"Yes, Mama. I rode down to the beach."

Lady Fairfax sighed.

"You know how I feel about that, Chiara, you seem to be going out of your way to make me unhappy."

"I don't mean to, Mama. It's just that I so love to ride."

"Oh, Chiara, that's the least of it. Elaine told me that you have been very rude to her brother this afternoon."

"I don't think I was rude, Mama. I simply told him that I did not wish to marry him and that he must not ask me again."

Lady Fairfax's eyebrows were raised in alarm.

"What has happened to you, Chiara? You never used to speak in such a bold outspoken way. I don't like it at all."

Chiara apologised and again told her Mama that she did not mean to upset her.

"But where are the Fulwells? I thought they would be sitting with you, as they usually do at this time."

"They are packing their things, Chiara. Poor Elaine is terribly distressed at your treatment of her brother."

"Oh – are they leaving?"

Chiara's heart gave a great bound of joy.

"Yes, they are. I have given them some money to go abroad and take a little holiday."

Chiara was very surprised to hear this, but before she could comment, Lady Fairfax's next words caused her to feel even more astonished.

"Elaine Fulwell really is such a generous woman, Chiara. I cannot quite believe it, but she has offered to take you with her."

"What! But – why? I don't understand!"

Chiara's happiness evaporated in an instant, as she imagined herself with Eglantine and Marigold, staying in a crowded boarding house on the coast of France.

"It is quite extraordinary that she should be so kind, after you have insulted and hurt her dear brother. But she insists that you should accompany them."

"Mama – I cannot think of anything I should hate more." Chiara cried. "Please, don't make me go!"

"My darling, you have behaved very badly. If Mrs. Fulwell has the generosity to forgive you, I don't think you are in a position to turn down her offer. And, to be frank, I am so upset with you that I shall be quite glad if you go away for a while and leave me to prepare for my wedding in peace."

Lady Fairfax's eyes were bright with tears.

"I had so hoped that we might have shared that very special day – "

Chiara's head was in a whirl of panic.

What if Mervyn Hunter was to follow them out to France – and renew his attentions to her? What would she do so far away from home and at the mercy of him and his relations?

But then all these thoughts vanished from her mind, as she heard her mother add,

"You had better go and look through your things, Chiara. St. Petersburg, I have heard, is a very fashionable place."

St. Petersburg!

A thrill of excitement passed through her body as she heard the name.

Surely St. Petersburg is the very place where Count Arkady Dimitrov lives and never in her wildest dreams had Chiara thought that she might ever go there.

"Of course, Mama," she answered, her dislike of Marigold, Eglantine and their mother completely forgotten. "I shall do so right away!"

CHAPTER NINE

At last Chiara was alone!

Mrs. Fulwell and her daughters had gone to a party and they had made no objection when she had asked if she might stay behind in the rented apartment that overlooked one of the beautiful canals that ran through St. Petersburg.

In point of fact, since they had arrived in Russia, they seemed to prefer it if she did not accompany them to the Society salons and other events to which Mrs. Fulwell had managed to arrange invitations almost every night.

"You must understand, my dear," she had said to Chiara on several occasions, "that I simply cannot allow you to spoil my girls' opportunities in any way. After all, we must remember how lucky you are. *You* have already had a very respectable proposal of marriage!"

And Chiara could not help smiling as she thought of the surprised expressions that greeted her introduction as 'Lady Chiara Fairfax'.

People at social functions did not expect someone like her, an aristocrat, to be travelling with the Fulwells and, quite often, they seemed very pleased to meet her and much more interested in talking to her than to Eglantine and Marigold.

But the one face that Chiara really longed to see and she looked out for every time she went to a *soirée* or a luncheon was never there. So she was quite happy to stay behind all on her own.

She went to the window of the apartment where she was staying with the Fulwells and with a great effort pulled up the heavy sash window so that she could lean out and watch the sunset turn the blue sky above St. Petersburg to glorious rose-pink.

A breath of cool evening air drifted up to her from the still water of the canal that led down to the River Neva.

St. Petersburg was not at all as Chiara had expected it to be. It was far more attractive than anything she could have imagined, with its endless Palaces and Cathedrals and expanses of glittering water.

At the same time it was almost like Venice, where her Mama and Papa had taken her as a child. Except that St. Petersburg was built on a much grander scale.

She had been staying there for several weeks now, but she felt as if she would never grow tired of gazing at the enchanting buildings all around her.

The nights were starting to draw out as the summer approached. It must be quite late now and yet the sun had only just set.

Chiara sighed with pleasure, feasting her eyes on the beauty of the darkening sky and let her mind drift back to the first day of the long voyage from England.

She had been sitting in the salon on board the ship, playing draughts with Marigold, who seemed to have no ability to amuse herself and must always be playing some game or other.

Eglantine was not far away, a pair of wire-rimmed glasses perched on her long nose as she perused the latest fashions in a magazine.

"Oh, it's so unfair! You've won again!" Marigold cried petulantly and pushed the board across the table.

"I'm sorry," Chiara said, "but that is just the way it turned out."

"You must apply yourself, Marigold. If you really concentrated on what you are doing, you would win easily. Draughts is a very simple game."

Without lifting her eyes from a magazine, Eglantine rebuked her sister.

"I hate it and what's more, I feel sick. Why do we have to make this stupid voyage to Russia anyway?"

Marigold got up and flounced away from the table.

"I'm going to the cabin to lie down."

Chiara wondered if she should follow her, to make sure that she was all right.

The ship was moving up and down over the waves quite strongly now and, though Chiara loved the sensation, she could imagine that others might find it unsettling.

"Oh, just leave her," Eglantine snapped. "She's always carrying on about something or other."

"So why did you choose St. Petersburg?" Chiara asked. "There are many lovely places easier to get to."

She had been wondering about this for some time, but in the frenzied excitement of packing and beginning the journey, she had never put her question into words.

"Oh! Don't you know?"

Eglantine looked up from her magazine and peered at Chiara over her glasses.

"We've been invited by a titled Russian gentleman and Mama thinks he may have taken a fancy to me."

Chiara felt a little rush of amusement, as a picture came into her mind of an elderly aristocrat, perhaps with bushy white side-whiskers, who had fallen helplessly under the spell of Eglantine's rather severe charms.

But her next words struck a chill into her heart.

"Count Arkady Dimitrov. You've met him, haven't you?"

"Yes – I have – "

Chiara strove to keep her voice from shaking.

"Mama says that he danced with you, just the once, at the Sandringham Ball. And then he cut you dead. Lady Fairfax told her so."

"Yes – but – " Chiara stopped herself.

At all costs, she must not let Eglantine know how she felt about Arkady.

"But he has always been perfectly charming to *me*. Such lovely manners."

Eglantine's nose was high in the air with pride and she raised her right hand to pat her fair hair, which had been elaborately curled for the journey.

"Have you – danced with him?"

Chiara could hardly say it, but she had to know.

"Oh, no, but Mama believes that he is completely smitten. He invited us to take Russian tea with him and paid particular attention to me the whole time."

Eglantine's gaze dropped to her magazine again.

Chiara's mind was in turmoil.

She simply could not believe that the dark-haired, proud Count, who had whirled her so swiftly and skilfully across the dance floor, who had spoken of the wild swans flying North and whose dark eyes had gazed into hers with such amazing fire and passion, could possibly be attracted to Eglantine.

And yet – he had invited them to St. Petersburg! Had he asked them to stay with him? Did he intend to propose to Eglantine?

It took all the self-control Chiara possessed to stay silent and ask no more questions as the ship ploughed on across the choppy waters of the North Sea.

When they finally arrived in Russia, her fears were somewhat allayed by the fact that Count Arkady Dimitrov was nowhere to be seen in St. Petersburg.

The Count was out of town and the servants at his Palace seemed to have no idea who Mrs. Fulwell was when they accepted her calling card.

She and her daughters called several times and left a number of messages, but still there was no reply and all the shutters at the many windows of the Palace remained closed.

The Count was not at home.

Surely that was not the behaviour of a man in love, Chiara thought and, as she leaned a little further out of the window and breathed in the sweet air of the evening, an eddy of hope swirled in her heart.

Every time she went out and walked in the elegant streets between the tall white Palaces and houses, she half expected, even though she knew he was away, to see the Count's tall elegant figure walking towards her and hear his wonderful resonant voice.

Surely she must meet him again sometime in this beautiful City, which she was growing to love so much.

"*Mademoiselle*, would you now care for some tea? The samovar is hot."

A soft voice with a strong Russian accent recalled Chiara from her reverie and she ducked back in through the window.

"Yes, thank you, Karine, I would."

Karine was a young Russian girl Mrs. Fulwell had employed to look after her daughters and attend to their clothes while they stayed at the apartment.

She was slight and slim with a long plait of ebony hair wound around her elegant small head.

"You are quiet tonight, *mademoiselle*," she said, as she brought Chiara a glassful of tea with a large slice of lemon floating in it. "You did not wish to go to the party?"

Chiara shook her head, whilst sipping the delicious, refreshing beverage. Tea with lemon was one of the things about life in Russia that she especially enjoyed.

"But, *mademoiselle*, I think you should take every opportunity to go out and really enjoy yourself while you are here. There is so much to do. Theatre, opera, ballet, the best in the world."

"I should love to go to the theatre, but Mrs. Fulwell says it is so difficult to buy tickets and she prefers, anyway, to go to places where she can meet people and mingle with Society."

Karine looked thoughtful.

"They will not be back for some time," she said. "I have an idea."

She leaned towards Chiara and whispered,

"I have a friend who can get me into the Maryinsky tonight – why don't you come with me!"

*

Chiara felt as if she had been holding her breath for the longest time, as she looked down from her little seat right at the back of the theatre and watched the beautiful spectacle that was unfolding on the stage.

A long line of white-clad dancers, their feather-like tutu skirts revealing slender graceful legs, tripped across the stage.

They were *swans*!

In their midst the Prima Ballerina, with a crown of sparkling diamonds nestling in her hair, raised her arms with a graceful gesture of delight, as she pirouetted across

127

the stage, flying to the loving embrace of the Prince who pursued her.

"Oh!" Chiara gave a sigh of disappointment as the music and lights died away and a heavy richly embroidered curtain fell, hiding the stage from the auditorium.

"It's over!"

"No, not at all." Karine smiled at her ignorance. "This is just the interval. There will be more, much more. Come, let's take a walk and stretch our legs."

Everywhere they went was crowded, thronged with bejewelled Russian ladies and their dark-suited husbands and escorts.

There was so much to look at that Chiara found it hard to concentrate, as Karine explained to her the story of the ballet *Swan Lake* and the beautiful Princess who has been turned into a swan by the evil magician, Rothbart.

"You know so much," she told Karine, as the two of them stepped out onto the street for some fresh air.

"Yes. I am a dancer," Karine replied and her pretty face looked drawn. "I should be here tonight, but my knee is not good. I fell in the performance one night as I ran off the stage and now I cannot dance."

"Oh, but that's terrible," Chiara exclaimed.

Now that Karine had said this, she realised that the girl was walking with a slight limp, although she disguised it very well.

Karine shrugged.

"I am lucky. I learned how to sew while I worked at the theatre. So, it's easy for me to find work with ladies like Madame Fulwell."

"You must miss the theatre so much and it must be so wonderful to dance like that on the stage and wear those lovely costumes."

"Yes, it is. I try not to think of it too much. But I am glad we came tonight. I knew you would like it."

Chiara was not listening.

Someone had come out of the front doors of the theatre.

A tall dark-haired man, who stood with his head thrown back, taking deep breaths of the sweet evening air.

It was the Count.

He must have returned to his Palace!

Chiara felt suddenly faint.

She and Karine were standing in the shadows at the side of the theatre out of the way of all the Society people, and, unless the Count came looking, he would not be able to see them.

"What is it?" the girl was asking. "You have seen someone?"

"No – no, it's nothing," Chiara replied.

She now remembered the morning after the ball at Sandringham, when the Count had suddenly appeared from the misty garden and come to her side.

Would he sense that she was here now and come over to her?

But he was turning back, already, to go inside. He had no idea that Chiara was standing so close to him, her heart beating so hard it felt as if it would leap out of her chest.

"Come, we should go back to our seats," Karine said and put her hand on Chiara's arm. "Are you all right, *mademoiselle*?"

Chiara nodded.

Sitting through the next act of the performance was agony for her. The Prince left the lake where the swans dwelled to return to his Palace and she waited eagerly for him to be reunited with the beautiful swan, Odette, so that they could dance together once more.

But instead an impostor came to the Court. A *Black Swan*. And she was the magician's evil daughter and she enchanted the Prince and then tricked him into promising himself to her.

The dancing was fabulous and Chiara had never seen anything like the passion with which the Black Swan, Odile, spun around and around, balancing upon her pointed toes.

But she could hardly bear to see the Prince spurn his true love.

When the next interval came, the two girls stayed in their seats.

"Karine – does this ballet have a happy ending?" Chiara asked. "Does he find the Swan Princess again?"

Karine gave a sad little smile.

"Yes, but he cannot be with her, as he has promised himself to the other one, the Black Swan. They can only be joined in death and they fall together into the lake."

Chiara's heart stung with sadness.

"Would you mind, awfully, if we left?" she asked. "I don't think I could bear to see it!"

Karine looked at her.

"Of course I don't mind – I have seen it a thousand times. But I am worried, you don't seem yourself?"

As they walked back to the apartment beneath the deep velvet blue of the night sky, Karine said,

"It's that gentleman, isn't it, who came out of the theatre? You have met him before. He has broken your heart!"

"I danced with him at a ball in England, but please, you must not say anything. You must forget all about it," Chiara's voice was trembling as she spoke.

"Oh, these gentlemen," Karine sighed. She slid her arm through Chiara's. "They don't know how much pain they cause! But don't despair, I am sure he will remember you when he sees you again."

Chiara did not know whether she wanted to see Arkady again or not. What if he did not remember her and the wonderful waltz they had shared? She did not think she could bear that.

*

A few days later a visitor was announced at the Fulwell's rented apartment.

Count Arkady Dimitrov, who had been resident at his country *Dacha* for so long, had come to call and to take tea with the ladies.

Chiara felt her face turn scarlet as she heard his name.

She was helping Karine to let out one of Marigold's dresses, a blue-and-green striped silk that the girl could no longer do up, since her passion for blinis with caviar and sour cream had caused her waistline to expand since they had arrived in Russia

What would the Count think of Chiara, if he found her like this, stitching away like a servant?

She did not mind helping Karine at all. It was fun to sit and talk about her days in the theatre, much more interesting than playing childish card games with Marigold or listening to Eglantine dissecting the latest fashions.

But the last time that the Count had seen her, she had been wearing the exquisite white ball gown with the blue sash.

"Out! Quickly!" Mrs. Fulwell snapped at the two of them. "I cannot have all this clutter in the parlour."

She chivvied Chiara and Karine to tidy away their work.

But the Count was already coming into the room.

"*Madame*!" he then bowed low over Mrs. Fulwell's hand. "It has been too long."

Chiara shivered at the sound of his deep voice, as she stood there, clutching Marigold's dress in her hands.

Now the two sisters were curtseying deeply with Eglantine hiding her glasses behind her back as she greeted the Count.

"Count Dimitrov. We should be so delighted if you would take a glass of tea with us. As you can see, Mama has invested in a samovar!" she said.

The Count smiled.

"Why ever not?" he replied. "You must be enjoying your stay in St. Petersburg, if you are embracing our local customs."

Mrs. Fulwell left her elder daughter to escort the Count to a chair. She came over to Chiara and told her in a fierce whisper to leave the room.

But she was too late.

The Count was frozen to the spot, all of Eglantine's words unheard.

He was staring at Chiara.

"*You*!" he exclaimed. "*But how can this be*?"

Chiara heard Karine catch her breath and felt the Russian girl's hand in the small of her back, softly pushing her forward.

But she was too overcome to speak. To have the Count so close to her was unbearable.

"This is Lady Chiara Fairfax – Count Dimitrov," Mrs. Fulwell said, speaking the words as quickly as she could and attempting to steer the Count away.

He stayed where he was.

"How good to see you again."

Once more, Chiara felt Karine nudge her.

She had to say something.

"Thank you – Count Dimitrov," she managed and forced her trembling limbs into a curtsey.

The Count waited for a moment, as if he was expecting her to say more, but she could only stand in front of him, looking at the polished toes of his gleaming boots and breathing in the strong scent of lime and spices she remembered so well.

Then Eglantine was pulling him away from her, leading him to a chair, telling him how much they had all missed him and how much more exciting their stay in St. Petersburg would be now that he had come.

Chiara sat there quietly in the corner listening to his voice and snatching a quick glance at his handsome face every now and again.

She almost wished that he had not come. For she had been so happy in St. Petersburg, so much so that the memory of him had diminished fractionally in her mind.

But now that he was in the same room, a strange wild feeling possessed her.

She longed for them to be alone together, for him to take her in his arms and dance with her.

And yet, if he did so, her joy would be so intense that she did not know if she could stand it.

She wished that she had not seen the tragic but beautiful ballet, the tale of the Swan Queen and her Prince, who could never be united except in death – for it had left a strange sense of panic and foreboding in her heart.

Now the Count, having sipped his tea, was standing up to leave.

"I have tickets for a performance of Anna Pavlova tonight and I wonder if you would care to join me?" he was saying to Mrs. Fulwell.

"Of course! It would be utterly delightful, would it not, Eglantine? How thoughtful of you, dear Count," Mrs. Fulwell spluttered. "My daughters and I would feel most privileged to attend the performance with you."

There was a pause and then the Count spoke again,

"Lady Chiara, would you not like to come too?" he said. "I have enough tickets. Do you care for the ballet?"

"Yes!" Chiara found her voice suddenly. "I do – I have seen *Swan Lake* – "

"What? When was this?" Mrs. Fulwell could not keep the anger out of her voice.

"Oh, then you will appreciate the divine Pavlova," The Count said. "You must join us."

Chiara looked up and saw that he was smiling at her and she remembered the look of roguish delight on his face when he had encountered her galloping on the beach.

"I should love to," she replied, as his glowing dark eyes looked deeply into hers.

And then he was gone and Chiara was left with trembling limbs to endure the incredulous anger of Mrs. Fulwell.

"What are you thinking of, Chiara? How many times have I told you that you must not interfere with my Eglantine's chances? You greedy thoughtless girl. Is it not enough for you that you have one delightful gentleman at your feet, who would do anything to make you his wife –

but you must go chasing after any eligible bachelor that walks through the door?"

"He asked her, Mama," Marigold pointed out.

"Oh, do be quiet!" Mrs. Fulwell snapped. "Well, my Lady, you had better mind your manners tonight and keep well out of the way or you will wish you had stayed at home."

"Really, Mama, don't fuss so," Eglantine piped up, putting her glasses back on. "The Count was just being polite in asking her. He hardly spoke a word to her all the time he was here, didn't you notice?"

It was true that Count Dimitrov had spent most of his time speaking to the Fulwells.

But Chiara's mind was full of the memory of the moment when his eyes looked straight into hers.

He had not forgotten her!

*

As soon as Anna Pavlova stepped into the circle of light on the great stage at the Maryinsky, Chiara knew that she was witnessing something very special.

The fragile ballerina with the slender neck and the enormous dark eyes had a magical quality of beauty and sadness.

Her performance was not of a full-length ballet, like *Swan Lake*, but a series of short vignettes.

Pavlova drifted like an autumn leaf, fluttered like a butterfly, pranced and twinkled as a Fairy doll and then, last but not least, she enacted her most famous role, *The Dying Swan.*

Chiara felt tears slip down her cheeks as soft sad cello music filled the theatre and the graceful white bird in front of her struggled over and over to fly away, but at the end sank to the stage to breathe her last.

When the performance came to an end, she rose to stumble out of her luxurious seat in the first circle of the auditorium, hanging her head so that her tearful face would not be noticed.

"What was that all about?" Eglantine said, as they stepped outside the theatre. "It was all very pretty, but I didn't quite get the point of it."

The Count raised his eyebrows.

"Pavlova is one the greatest artists to come out of Russia," he pronounced in a tone of surprise.

"Yes, but what was the story?" Marigold asked. "It just looked like a lot of dancing around to me."

"I don't think there was meant to be a story – " Chiara found herself saying, "it was more – of a feeling."

"Or maybe," the Count came in, "the greatest story of all – the story of life and the struggle against death."

The sombre tone of his voice as he said these words sent a thrill through Chiara that seemed to chill her and yet warm her all at the same time.

Suddenly she did not care whether he saw her tear-stained cheeks.

But he was not looking at her. He was raising his hand and hailing a carriage.

"Mrs. Fulwell," he said. "Thank you very much for your company tonight. My coachman is here, let him take you and your charming daughters back to your apartment."

"Why, Count! What a privilege indeed – we are quite overcome. But will you not be joining us?"

"I prefer to walk," he replied.

He turned to Chiara, fixing his dark eyes on hers and spoke in a low voice,

"The white nights of St, Petersburg are almost upon us now that summer begins. There is still light in the sky.

It would be a great pleasure for me to share a little of this beautiful evening with you, my English angel."

Then he raised his voice loudly and clearly so that Mrs. Fulwell could not fail to hear him,

"Lady Chiara, will you please do me the honour of walking with me?"

Chiara's heart took wing with joy.

At that moment she forgot everything but the man who stood before her, his voice still filling her ears.

"Yes!" she replied. "I should – love to!"

CHAPTER TEN

The carriage then rattled away, bearing the Fulwells back to their apartment and the Count took Chiara's arm and began to walk.

She was giddy with joy.

As she felt his warm strong body pressing against her arm, she was filled with the same spinning, delicious sensation she had felt in the ballroom at Sandringham.

They strolled along gleaming canals and the bright lights in the windows of Palaces shone out to be reflected in the water below.

Above their heads, the sky was an extraordinary and brilliant shade of royal blue.

"What is it?" the Count asked, as Chiara drew a long shivering breath of delight.

"Look – a star is coming out and it is still as light as day!" she cried, gazing at the sky.

"Are you afraid that I will keep you out too late?" he said, looking down at her. "I promise that you will be home long before all the stars have appeared – "

Chiara could not help blushing.

She wanted to say that she was happy to walk with him for as long as he wished – for the whole night, even, but instead she asked,

"Tell me – why did you say the *white* nights of St. Petersburg. Tonight the sky – is blue. The bluest blue I – have ever seen."

He laughed at her words.

"It is not yet the time of the white nights. That is at midsummer. And, I suppose that the sky is blue then too, but there is a lightness, a whiteness even that glows on the horizon at midnight."

"But – why?"

"St. Petersburg is so far to the North," he replied. "Our winters may be bitter, but at the height of summer the sun lingers in the sky all night."

"I should love to see it," Chiara sighed. "This City is the most beautiful place – I have ever been."

He did not reply, but she felt his gaze on her and the pressure of his dark eyes looking down.

"Why have you come here?" he asked her.

Chiara's mind was in turmoil.

What should she tell him? She could not speak of her problems with Mervyn Hunter.

"My Mama – sent me – " she said after a moment.

"Whatever for?" the Count sounded incredulous. "And why should your mother give Mrs. Fulwell and her silly daughters the pleasure of your company, when she might have you at home with her?"

"She – is getting married, and – she felt it would be better if I went away for a little while."

The Count shook his head.

"I cannot fathom it, but her loss is my gain."

Chiara's heart gave a little leap as she felt him press her arm closer to him.

He carried on speaking,

"I must say, I spent some time with the Fulwells in London and I find them amusing, but – "

"They are odd, aren't they?" Chiara said, greatly relieved that he was no longer questioning her. "They did not seem to appreciate the dancing tonight. It was so sad – and yet so beautiful – the swan dying – "

"Oh, you have it perfectly. I think you understand the beauty and the soul of our Russian artists."

"Yes – I – " Chiara began.

But the words were snatched from her, as the Count drew her close to him.

She felt the urgency and the depth of the passion that surged in him, yet she was not afraid, and she raised her face to his and felt his lips press softly against hers in a kiss that seemed to her to come straight from Heaven.

They stood perfectly still by the black waters of the canal, yet Chiara's spirit was flying, soaring up into the deep blue of the sky, as the Count's tender kisses filled her soul with enchantment.

"I cannot believe that you are not an angel, but just a lovely mortal girl," he whispered and she felt his warm breath against her hair as he released her.

"I am – just a girl," she said, "but I feel as if I could fly away – "

"Don't!" he asserted, his voice deep. "Stay a little longer, please!"

A flame of exquisite anticipation lit in Chiara's heart as she waited for him to kiss her again, but instead he took her arm and they walked on.

"I must remember that you are *just a girl*! A girl who is out very late with a man she scarcely knows. And I shall now deliver you safely to your apartment," he said, quickening his pace a little.

"Oh, I wish – " a bleak despair filled Chiara's heart, as she realised that their walk was almost over.

"So do I!" he said, speaking her very thought. "If only we could walk on through the night and then fly away together. But – will you promise to walk with me again? May I see you, while you stay in St. Petersburg?"

"Of course!" Chiara murmured.

And, as he heard this, the Count caught her in his arms again and held her to his heart, so that she felt the power of his love flow into her, lighting her so that her soul shone like that single star above them.

*

"My dear Count! How kind of you to bring her Ladyship back to us so promptly!"

Mrs. Fulwell had a wide smile on her plump fair face as she stood in the hall of the rented apartment, but her eyes were as hard as stones.

She reached out and laid a hand on his arm.

"A word, if I may?"

Arkady was ready to leave.

Chiara had been hustled off to her room and there was no reason at all for him to stay, but Mrs. Fulwell was determined to speak to him.

"I really must apologise, Count Dimitrov, for Lady Chiara's behaviour."

"Please, Mrs. Fulwell, do not distress yourself, I – "

He could scarcely get the words out, as she was still chattering at him.

"No, but you must understand what kind of a young woman she is! Shameless! Her mother asked me to take over the supervision of her, so there would be no repetition of what happened in the spring."

In spite of himself, Arkady's curiosity was aroused.

What was she referring to?

"She, oh, I can hardly bring myself to speak of it! She led my dear brother, Mervyn, to think that she cared for him – they were as good as engaged. Oh, yes, she led him on! Smiles, kisses, all manner of inducements – "

The pleasure and beauty of the exquisite night, of the glorious embrace, of the sweet kiss that had filled him with almost unbearable joy, were shattered for Arkady.

Another man and one of those boorish Englishmen probably, who had been pursuing her at Sandringham, had kissed his divine angel's lips, held her in his arms.

Mrs. Fulwell was far from finished,

"And now, my dear Count – she cannot rest but she is trying to steal from my own darling girls any man who shows an interest in them. She is a selfish hussy. I should hate to think that you wasted even a second of your time on such a creature."

Her voice was soft now and the pressure of her hand on his arm insistent.

Arkady felt sick. His joy was broken, crushed and flung to the ground like a wounded bird.

He shook Mrs. Fulwell's hand from his arm and strode to the door of the apartment, not even pausing to bow or to take his leave.

He did not wish to spend another moment in this false unpleasant world, where nothing was as it seemed.

*

"But – I don't understand. You wish me to leave?"

Chiara looked down at the boat tickets that Mrs. Fulwell had just thrust into her hand.

"Today, if you don't mind!"

Mrs. Fulwell pulled off her cloak and threw it on the sofa. She had been out at the break of day to arrange for Chiara's journey back to England.

"Why?"

"I am very surprised you need to ask me that," Mrs. Fulwell growled and then she turned and snapped at her younger daughter,

"Marigold, get back to your room! I will not have your innocent ears corrupted by what I have to say."

Chiara reeled with horror as she listened to Mrs. Fulwell's words.

She was a wicked, selfish girl, deliberately trying to steal Eglantine's suitor, seducing him just as she had her dear brother.

But this time she would not get away with it, as the Count knew everything now and he was disgusted to know what kind of girl he had been consorting with last night.

Mrs. Fulwell spat out one last vicious sentence and then seized Chiara by the elbow.

"Go and pack!" she shouted. "Your boat leaves in three hours!"

Chiara's face was wet with tears as she stumbled into her small bedroom.

Karine was there, standing beside the bed.

"Oh, *mademoiselle*. I could not help overhearing, I am so sorry."

Sobs broke in Chiara's throat and she could not speak.

Karine's eyes were filling with tears too.

"I would do *anything* for you, *mademoiselle*, if I could help."

Chiara sat on the bed and fought to gain control of herself.

"I cannot bear that – he should think ill of me," she stammered. "But what can I do? She has filled his ears – with such poison."

"Go to him, *mademoiselle!*"

Chiara shook her head, blinking away tears.

"He will not believe me, after what she has said – and the boat leaves so soon – I must pack. Oh, but I don't want to leave – "

Karine sat beside her and took her hand.

"If only I might come with you, it is such a long journey for you to make alone."

Chiara clung tightly onto her hand and felt a little steadiness return to her.

"Karine – why don't you? I have some money that Mama has given me and I have spent almost nothing since I have been here. Come too!"

Karine's brown eyes lit up and she gave a joyful exclamation in Russian.

Then she added,

"I shall! The Fulwells care nothing for me, they will soon find another servant. But – "

Suddenly she looked very thoughtful,

"I have a little errand to run before I can go."

"Of course," Chiara said. "But – do be quick! The boat leaves very soon."

Karine vanished, disappearing through the door in a swift graceful movement and Chiara began, with a heavy heart, to put her things together for the long voyage home.

*

The bright sun of early summer blazed down over the front of Rensham Hall as Chiara stepped out of the hired chaise.

Even though it was almost noon, the shutters were closed and there was no sign of life anywhere.

"So this is your home," Karine said, her eyes wide as she gazed up at the row of tall windows.

Chiara nodded, trying not to feel anxious.

She went up to the front door and pushed it, but it was firmly closed. She turned the iron handle that rang a bell inside the hall.

Where was her Mama?

Had she not received the note that Chiara wrote to her just before she embarked on the voyage home?

Why was everything so still and quiet?

There was a crunch of footsteps on the gravel and Chiara turned round, her heart in her mouth, half expecting to see Mervyn Hunter bearing down upon them, but it was only Jonah, running from the stable yard to greet them, his thatch of fair hair flopping over his eyes.

"Lady Chiara!" he called out. "You're back!"

Relief flooded through Chiara at the sight of his familiar friendly face.

"Where is everyone?" she asked.

"Don't you know?" Jonah frowned in puzzlement. "I thought they'd written to you in Russia."

"What is it?"

Chiara felt suddenly faint with fear.

Had something happened to her Mama?

"Sad news," Jonah began and he suddenly grinned. "but happy too!"

Chiara was thoroughly confused and she begged him to tell more.

"Lord Darley's brother passed away," he said, "and her Ladyship has gone to be with him in Pembrokeshire."

"Oh."

Chiara breathed out in a long sigh as the meaning of his words became clear.

Everything was all right.

Mama was safe. The letter she wrote must have arrived in St. Petersburg after Chiara's hasty departure.

"And – Mr. Hunter?"

Chiara's heart gave a flutter of anxiety as she spoke his name.

Now Jonah was smiling broadly.

"Oh, Mr. Hunter is gone with them, my Lady. Lord Darley will give his racehorses a home, now that the estate is his as he inherits it from his brother."

So she would be free of Mervyn Hunter at last!

She noticed that Jonah was eyeing her companion with some curiosity.

"Jonah, this is Miss Karine Federova from the Russian Imperial Ballet."

Jonah ducked his head shyly.

"Pleased to meet you, miss."

There was a noise of bolts being pulled and the front door of Rensham Hall then opened slowly to reveal a surprised-looking butler.

"Lady Chiara!" he cried. "We were not expecting you. Welcome!"

As Chiara stepped into the hall, she saw, among the pile of letters that lay on the hall table, her own note with its Russian stamp and postmark.

Her Mama must have left for Pembrokeshire before it arrived.

*

There was something idyllic about the summer days that followed at Rensham Hall.

146

Lady Fairfax remained in Wales, as her wedding would take place there, now that Lord Darley had come into the estate.

Chiara was to join them in a few weeks' time to carry out her duties as bridesmaid, but until then she stayed alone at home, looked after by the familiar servants and with Karine for company.

There was no one to pester her and no one to tell her what to do and she was totally free to pass all her time enjoying herself.

But for all that, it was not a happy time for her.

She tried hard to ignore the deep painful sadness that lay in her heart as she walked in the garden or rode Erebus in the Park.

She could not bear to go further afield on her little pony, for he would always want to head for the beach and the sea and she could not endure to go there anymore.

The memory of her first meeting with the Count there in that lonely wild place where the sky met the sea was now mingled with the sweet recollection of their walk through the St. Petersburg night.

And the pain of knowing that he must now hate and despise her and never wish to see her again cut her like a knife.

But the garden was full of June roses and the sweet scent of cut hay filled the air and Chiara did her best to seem cheerful and bright.

*

"*Mademoiselle*, I would like to ask a great favour of you," Karine said to her one afternoon, as they sat in the garden, passing the long sunny interval between luncheon and tea.

"Of course. Anything, Karine," Chiara replied.

Sometimes, since she had returned home, she had wished that Elizabeth was still in Ely and not far away on the other side of the world with her new husband in the hot climate of India.

She longed to tell Elizabeth about the Count and share with her dear friend the feelings of ecstasy and pain that tormented her, whenever she thought about him.

Somehow, it was not the same trying to put it all in a letter, knowing that it would be many weeks before the envelope arrived and Elizabeth would be able to read her words.

But she was very glad that Karine had come back to England with her.

For, although they never spoke of the Count, Chiara often caught the Russian's brown eyes watching her, when she was feeling particularly sad and the fact that Karine knew how she was feeling was a comfort.

Now her eyes were shining, as she told Chiara,

"Jonah wants to teach me how to ride."

"What a good idea!" Chiara exclaimed.

Although he often seemed shy and uncomfortable in her company, Jonah had developed a great liking for the Russian girl.

He had been supplying armfuls of fresh comfrey from the garden so that Chiara might make poultices for Karine's injured knee and his face shone with pleasure when he saw, after only a very few days, that Karine was walking without any limp at all.

"But I wonder if we might borrow your pony?" Karine was saying. "Jonah says he is the best one to teach me."

"Oh, Goodness! He can be very lively at times."

Chiara could not help a little stab of jealousy at the

thought of sharing her precious Erebus, but she did not want to disappoint Karine, so she added,

"Of course, if Jonah says so, then you must borrow him."

Karine's face broke into a joyful smile.

"And please, you must come and help me. I have never done this before."

Chiara need not have worried that Karine might not be able to manage Erebus. Her training as a dancer had given her such balance and lightness that the little pony did not bat an eyelid when she jumped up onto his back.

He pricked his ears and trotted swiftly around the paddock and Karine sat up very straight and looked most elegant as her body swayed gracefully with his movements.

Jonah's face grew pink with pride as they circled around him, whilst Karine was laughing with delight at the unaccustomed sensation of sitting on a spirited horse.

Chiara smiled and clapped her hands to encourage them, but inside she felt very cold and alone.

Erebus seemed to love having the Russian girl ride him. Perhaps he would give all his affection and loyalty to her now.

'I have nothing,' she thought. 'No one cares for me, I am alone in the world.'

Erebus came to a sudden halt, his head high in the air and Karine, taken by surprise, tumbled from the saddle.

She was so agile and quick that she twisted in the air and landed on her feet, laughing, as Jonah ran to her.

"Are you – all right?" he stammered, his Norfolk accent thicker than ever in his distress.

"But of course," Karine teased him.

She slid out of Jonah's anxious hands and leapt up into the saddle again.

This time, she did not stay seated, but tucked her legs under her so that she was kneeling.

Then, suddenly, she was standing up in the saddle and Chiara caught her breath as Karine held out her arms and raised one slender leg high in the air behind her.

It was a pose quite as lovely as anything she had seen on the great stage of the Maryinsky in St. Petersburg.

"My knee is strong again!" Karine cried.

The coldness in Chiara's heart melted as she saw the elation on the girl's face.

Then Erebus threw up his head, his ears pricked as he gazed at something in the distance and Karine dropped gracefully to the ground.

"Someone's comin'," Jonah said. "Looks like an old chap, come seekin' work. I'll go speak to him."

Then he headed off towards a bent ragged figure, wobbling up the drive on a battered bicycle.

"I suppose now that you will want to go back to St. Petersburg – to the theatre," Chiara quizzed Karine.

Karine shook her head, but her eyes looked sad and Chiara knew that she was torn between wanting to stay and longing to go back to the life that she loved.

"My Lady," Jonah came back, sounding flustered. "The man says he must speak to you. I told him to find the gardener and ask if there are any odd jobs, but he wouldn't listen."

The ragged bicyclist was now standing underneath a chestnut tree, staring at her, a grubby cap pulled down over his eyes.

He looked very disreputable.

"Shall I ask the butler to come, *mademoiselle*, and send him away?" Karine asked.

"No," Chiara replied. "I shall deal with it."

She felt nervous as she approached the unkempt man, as his face was smudged with dirt and he was staring at her intently, but somehow her feet kept walking towards him.

As she stepped under the green leaves of the tree, he swept off his cap and a lock of dark hair fell over his forehead.

"So, you are still speaking to me – " he began.

It was the Count.

Chiara's hands flew up to her throat, as she choked with shock and emotion.

"Why did you run away?" he asked, twisting the cap in his hands. "I came back to the apartment to find you, after your friend spoke to me – and you were gone!"

"My – friend?" Chiara managed to say.

"Yes – the dancer."

The Count glanced in the direction of Karine.

"The Russian girl."

So that was the errand that Karine had carried out just before they joined the ship. She had gone to the Count to speak on Chiara's behalf – to tell him the truth!

"Why did *you* not come?" he was asking, his deep voice making her tremble with its intensity.

"I thought that – you would not – believe me – "

Chiara felt a single hot tear slide down her cheek.

"I was angry, yes, bitterly angry, when I thought that you might have played false with me, but if you had come yourself, how could I have not believed you?"

"I am so – sorry," Chiara stammered, as shame and confusion overwhelmed her.

Why had she not trusted him? If she had gone to

him then and there and tried to explain, she might still be in St. Petersburg now.

He then stepped towards her and her body and soul expanded with happiness.

He was going to take her in his arms.

But he suddenly halted and stood in front of her, a doubtful expression on his face.

"I cannot – kiss you in this coat," he said, looking down at his torn and greasy sleeves.

Chiara's tears melted into laughter.

"Of course you can," she exclaimed. "I love your disguise! I still have the other old coat you wore when we first met. It's my most treasured possession!"

Now the Count threw back his head and laughed too and caught her in his arms.

"My beautiful glorious angel," he sighed, his breath warm against her hair. "That more than any words of love tells me that you care for me."

Chiara lay against him, filled with a bliss that was as warm and bright as the summer day glowing all around them.

She thrilled at the thought that he might kiss her, but instead, he took her shoulders in his strong hands and held her a little away from him, his face now drawn and tense.

"I have come," he said, "to ask you to marry me. I am dressed as a beggar, oh – partly because I feared that if Arkady Dimitrov came knocking at your door, you would turn him away. But, also, because I am so utterly humble before you, my darling. My love for you makes me always a beggar at your feet."

He let go of her and flung himself to his knees, his head hanging.

"Don't, please don't!"

Chiara touched his head and felt the softness of his dark hair under her fingers.

"You must not beg! I am – yours. I have always been. I love and adore you, Arkady, and will for eternity."

She knelt down with him, under the tree and put her arms around him and then he raised his head.

At last his lips were on hers in the tender kiss she had craved for so long.

*

Six months later a dazzle of twinkling stars shone down on the Count and Countess Dimitrov, as their troika sped through a forest not far from St. Petersburg.

Three elegant black thoroughbreds snorted as they raced across the sparkling snow, pulling their illustrious cargo as fast as they possibly could, their breath making a pale cloud in the icy night air.

"We are flying!" Chiara whispered, peering out of her fur-lined hood as the tall fir trees whisked by.

"Oh, this is sheer Heaven and I love you with all my heart and soul, my wonderful husband."

"So – you are not sorry that I did not take you to Paris for our honeymoon, my adorable angel?"

"No! I love it here – so much."

"You will not miss your home?"

"Of course I will – but Mama is married now. She is so happy in Pembrokeshire – and Rensham Hall is there for us to visit whenever we like."

"I should love that and we will gallop on the wild sands of Norfolk until we fly up to Heaven and I can tell God how much I love you!"

Arkady transferred the reins of the troika to one hand, so that he could slip his arm under his wife's thick

153

cloak and hold her to him.

"But you have given your heart to Russia now?"

Chiara closed her eyes, picturing the brightly-lit streets of St. Petersburg, glowing under their white blanket of snow.

She thought of all the rooms in the glorious white-and-gilt Palace that now were hers to roam and explore as she chose.

She saw again the packed theatre they had just left and her dearest friend Karine, pirouetting across the stage with exquisite grace, her eyes glancing up to the back of the gallery, where her young English fiancé, Jonah, was watching her, his heart aflame with love and admiration.

And she turned to her husband and replied,

"I love Russia," she said. "But my heart belongs to you, Arkady. Wherever you are, whatever happens to us, my heart belongs to you. When I am with you, I am in Heaven."